"*Side by Side* is a beautifully told story that shares not only a glimpse into the reality of many Muslims who come to Christ (especially in Muslim nations), but the passion and struggles of those who follow God's call to foreign countries. Set in the amazing, yet difficult landscape that is Sudan, it also provides readers with an opportunity to meet the people and experience the culture that few have been blessed to know firsthand. Compelling and fast moving, I couldn't help devouring it in a day! I look forward to reading it again and again as well as share it others!"

—JAMI BELEW, event manager, Women of Faith

"*Side by Side* by Jana Kelley is an insightful and encouraging look at the lives of Christians living and working overseas and how God can use them to carry out His purposes among the people there. I was captivated!"

—ELAINE MEADOR, wife of executive advisor to the president,
International Mission Board

"Jana's novel gives insight into just how difficult it is for anyone who forms part of the majority religion of a country like Sudan to journey in finding Jesus. Yet, that miracle does happen! The book has a wonderful line of tension to keep the reader fascinated right to the end. A well-worth read. Highly recommended!"

—NORMAN JOHNSON, Sudan Support Network, South Africa

"I absolutely love this book. I actually wept as I came to the end of it. *Side by Side* captivated my thoughts for days. I wanted to read more of Mia's and Halimah's story."

—LOIS ROBINETTE, WMU director of Tabernacle Baptist Church

"Compelling and compassionate, fascinating and frightening, Jana Kelley masterfully unfolds a complex and gripping story depicting real life on the mission field. The good and the bad, the mundane and magnificent—all have a place in this novel about how God uses an ordinary young couple to reach Muslims for Christ. Anyone interested in cross-cultural ministry or missions will be greatly helped and blessed by this book. I will require all of my students to read *Side by Side* by Jana Kelley."

—ROBIN DALE HADAWAY, ThD, DMin, professor of missions,

vice president for institutional initiatives,

Midwestern Baptist Theological Seminary

"*Side by Side* is a beautiful story of faith and courage in missions. Jana does a superb job transporting the reader to Muslim soil and introducing them to the wonder, challenges, and realities of life there. Jana's characters come face-to-face with who they really are in trying circumstances and learn to overcome their personal biases, to embrace truth and pursue joy."

—DICK AND JENNIFER BROGDEN, lifelong friends

of the Kelleys in North Africa

side by side

inspired by real-life events

A NOVEL

JANA KELLEY

NEW HOPE®
PUBLISHERS
Gospel-Centered. Missions-Driven.

BIRMINGHAM, ALABAMA

New Hope® Publishers
PO Box 12065
Birmingham, AL 35202-2065
NewHopeDigital.com
New Hope Publishers is a division of WMU®.

New Hope Publishers serves its authors as they express their views,
which may not express the views of the publisher.

Library of Congress Product Control Number   2014957545

Interior Designer: Glynese Northam

ISBN-13: 978-1-59669-430-9

N154109 • 0515 • 3M1

DEDICATION

Dedicated to the real Halimah.

ACKNOWLEDGMENTS

Thank You to God, who allows us to be part of His magnificent story. From the beginning to the end of this project, God opened and closed doors and showed the path to take. I am so grateful for His guidance all along the way.

To my husband, *Kris,* and our sons, *Aaron, Seth,* and *Joel:* we walked this road together in reality and then through fiction. Thank you for encouraging me to write. *Mom* and *Dad,* thank you for proofreading early manuscripts and praying. *Lois,* thank you for being my cheerleader. We've come a long way since sitting in a Sunday School room punching holes into home-made devotional books!

John and *Jenny Brady,* thank you for advocating for the writing of this book. I appreciate you. *Edna Ellison,* thank you for looking beyond what the manuscript was and seeing what it could be. *Andrea Mullins,* thank you for believing in the story enough to take a chance. *Joyce Dinkins,* thank you for not giving up. *Natalie Hanemann,* your perspective as an American wife and mother and your talent as an editor helped me improve the telling of this story. Thank you.

To all the people at *New Hope Publishers,* who have worked with me to shape and polish this novel, thank you. You have helped to make a dream come true.

Many people walked alongside me in various ways during the writing of this book. Because of that, I feel like this is a group project. To all of you who gave an encouraging word, advocated for the message of this book, prayed, and in many other ways helped to get us closer to the goal: thank you for being in the group.

GLOSSARY

abaya. A robe-like type of clothing worn by women.

Ahlan wa Sahlan. You are welcome (to come in, make yourself welcome, etc.)

Aleykum wassalaam. Response to "*Salaam aleykum.*"

Alhamdullilah. Allah.

Allah yabarak feek. Allah's blessing on you.

aseeda. A thick porridge-like food eaten with *kisra,* a paper-thin bread.

bakhoor. Incense.

bismillah. In the name of Allah.

dakwa. Sudanese peanut butter.

dallooka. A Sudanese drum.

dukhaan. Traditional incense "smoked" into women's skin.

Eid al-Adha. Festival of Sacrifice.

Eid al-Fitr. Festival at the end of Ramadan.

Eid Mubarak. Greeting for festivals. Literally: Happy Festival.

FGM. Female genital mutilation, female circumcision.

habeebtee. (Feminine) My dear.

Haboba. Grandmother.

halawa. A sugar mixture used for hair removal.

hosh. The enclosed outside area of Sudanese home.

'iftaar. Breakfast; breaking of the fast during Ramadan.

Injil. The New Testament.

insha' Allah. Literally, If Allah wills.

Isa. Jesus.

Isa alMasih. Jesus the Messiah.

jallabeeya. A white robe worn by Northern Sudanese men.

jinjaweed. Men in the Darfur region of Sudan who are armed
with guns.

jirtik. Part of a Northern Sudanese marriage ceremony.

khalwa. A Muslim school for intense religious training.

khawadja. Foreigner or white person.

kifta. A meat dish.

kisra. A paper-thin bread eaten with *aseeda*.

La illah 'ila Allah. A portion of the statement of faith for
Muslims: "There is no god but Allah."

Mabrook. Congratulations.

marara. A specialty dish in Sudan; raw sheep organs (mostly
liver).

Masa 'ilxayr. Good afternoon.

masha' Allah. Thanks to Allah.

muezzin. The person who calls the faithful to prayer from the
mosque, usually broadcast over loudspeakers.

Qur'an. The main Islamic holy book (also spelled by Westerners
as Koran or Quran).

Salaam aleykum. An Arabic greeting. Peace be upon you.

salata aswad. A Sudanese eggplant dip.

salon. A seating area for guests.

sambosa. A fried meat or vegetable pie.

shawarma. A meat wrap sandwich.

sheikh. Leader at a mosque.

shihada. The statement of faith for Muslims. Saying the *shihada*
is one of the five pillars of Islam.

shnoo. What?

shukran. Thank you.

souq. An open-air market.

subhia. The Northern Sudanese bridal dance ceremony.

sura. A section of the Qur'an.

tarha. A headscarf worn by Sudanese girls.

tayib. Good.

tobe. A colorful full-body scarf worn by married women in
    Sudan.

'utfudul. 'utfuduli (feminine). *'utfudulu* (plural). Used in various
    situations to mean welcome or help yourself.

'ukhti. My sister.

wudhu. Ceremonial washing before Muslim prayers.

ya'ateeki al-afeeya (feminine). An Arabic blessing meaning Allah
    give you health.

zibeeb. A raisin. Also the name of a bruise on the forehead
    caused by bowing forcefully to the ground during
    prayer.

Remember those earlier days after you had received the light, when you stood your ground in a great contest in the face of suffering. Sometimes you were publicly exposed to insult and persecution; at other times you stood side by side with those who were so treated. You sympathized with those in prison and joyfully accepted the confiscation of your property, because you knew that you yourselves had better and lasting possessions.

—HEBREWS 10:32–34

PROLOGUE

"You're moving to . . . Sudan?"

"Yes, Mom. Sudan." Mia put the last dinner plate in the dishwasher and then joined her mother at the kitchen table.

"I've heard they have a lot of orphanages." Her mother's cheery voice squeaked a little higher than usual, as if she were forcing the words out.

"That's South Sudan. North Sudan is a different country altogether." Mia willed her voice to remain calm. She had to be patient. This news was a lot for her parents to take in.

"And you say you'll live in . . . Khartoum?"

"Yes. Khartoum. That's the capital city." Mia wondered how Michael was doing with her father in the living room. She absently twisted a blonde curl between her fingers and looked at her mother's strained face.

"That can't be right, honey. I've read about Khartoum in the news. That's where the terrorists are. It's a dangerous place. Ask Michael again. Maybe you misunderstood."

"Mom, Michael and I made this decision together. I don't need to check with him. He will be working as the project manager at the head office in Khartoum as well as in the displacement camps just outside of the city. A lot of families who had to escape war-torn areas in Sudan moved to Khartoum. They live in these camps as refugees."

"Tell me again why it has to be Sudan."

Mia had to hand it to her mom for at least trying to understand. "Kellar Hope Foundation is an organization that helps families all over the world. Sudan is just one of them. The office in Sudan really needs someone gifted in management. The projects are suffering because they are so unorganized. With his skills, Michael is the perfect candidate for the job."

Mia leaned across the table and took her mother's hand. "You know how Michael and I have wanted to live overseas, have even felt like God wants us to help people in countries less developed than ours. Well, there aren't many countries less developed than Sudan, I guess." Mia grinned, hoping it was contagious.

Her mother remained serious, her expression distant, like she was contemplating something important.

"But what about the terrorists in North Sudan?"

"Mom, there are terrorists everywhere, even in America." Mia glanced toward the small television on the kitchen counter, where she often watched nightly news containing reports of terror threats in the United States.

"But Mia, the children. It isn't safe for them. Would you consider leaving them here with your father and me?"

"Mom!" Mia laughed nervously. Surely she wasn't serious. "We are taking the children. We are *moving* there."

"But . . . but . . . why risk your life?"

"It's an opportunity to help hurting people. We'll get to be a light for Jesus. Doesn't that make it worth it?"

"You can be a light for Jesus in Texas, Mia. You don't have to go to Africa for that. There are plenty of lost people right in your own neighborhood."

Mia realized that her mother was quoting the things her Sunday School class would say to her next week when she told them her daughter was moving to Africa. *But why didn't she understand that a move like this was bound to happen?*

Michael had worked at the home office for Kellar Hope since he and Mia married eight years ago. They believed in the vision of the small organization: to reach into challenged communities to help children and their families improve their lives. After years of enabling others to travel abroad to live and work, Michael had finally been given the opportunity. They wouldn't pass it up. It was almost like being missionaries . . . but not.

"Come, Mom. I'll show you where Khartoum is." Mia led her to the map she and Michael had hung on the wall of the kitchen. She placed her finger on Texas. "Here's where we are." Then she ran her finger from Texas all the way across to North Africa. "There, that's where Khartoum, Sudan is. Right on the Nile River."

Mia watched her mom, who was staring at the map. Was she trying to calculate how many thousands of miles apart they would be? Surely she knew this would eventually happen. Michael and Mia had often talked about their desire to work overseas.

Perhaps, like Mia, her mother had never considered Sudan a possibility. But, now their dream was a reality and that reality would be in Sudan. Mia twisted another stray curl around her finger as she stared at the map with her mom.

She hoped she was right that it would all be worth it.

❖ CHAPTER I ❖

Six months later.

Mia's back throbbed as she dumped the last bucket of dirty mop water into the open gutter in her front yard. She was only thirty. Why was her back aching so? She watched as the chocolate-colored water and yellow foam sloshed down the cement passage and slurped as it disappeared into the drain. How had the floors become so dirty? Mia was accustomed to cleaning her own house, but back in Texas she only used a mop in the kitchen and not very often at that.

Sighing, Mia rinsed the mop under an outside faucet and thought its raggedy strings looked like muddy dreadlocks. She grinned. People back home thought she was living such a strange and exotic life. If only they could see this. Daily life—no matter where a person lived—was not very glamorous. Dust and sweat collected on her brow. She never wore make-up (why take the time to apply something that would immediately melt off?), and she hated the clothes she wore. A woman shouldn't hate her outfits. Mia had quickly grown tired of the long skirts and long-sleeved blouses that living in a Muslim culture mandated. She would have relished just one day in a worn-out pair of blue jeans and a t-shirt.

It wasn't just the heat and clothes. A spiritual oppression hung like a fog over the city. Every time she drove to the grocery store, she would pass an enormous sign that screamed down to every car that passed by, "If anyone desires a religion other than Islam, never will it be accepted of him; and in the Hereafter he will be in the ranks of those who have lost (Qur'an 3:85)." She was a tiny grain of sand in a giant desert. How could she ever make a difference?

Mia's biggest competition for her attention, though, was motherhood. She spent most of her days in her house: potty training two-year-old Dylan, teaching four-year-old Annie her numbers, and helping Corey with his first grade homework. Couldn't she do those same things in the comfort of her own home back in Texas? Mia nurtured a spark deep in her soul: the conviction that God had a plan for her family and that plan involved Sudan. But it was only a spark and Mia calculated that it wouldn't be long before being the mother of three small children in this foreign land would snuff it out.

She propped the dripping mop against the outer wall next to the faucet. The heat would whisk away all the moisture in less than an hour. She turned around to survey the front yard. A cement privacy wall enclosed the house and yard, just like every other residence in Khartoum. A rectangular patch of grass in the front afforded an area large enough for the kids to run and play.

Near the outer wall, a lime tree, a mango tree, and several beautiful rose bushes flourished in spite of the desert climate. The roses were dark red, like the roses Michael had given her when he proposed. Mia smiled at the memory. They were college students back then and very much in love. Michael studied international business and his life dream was to work overseas. One day, he gave Mia seven roses and said, "No matter which of the seven continents we live on, I'll love you forever."

Michael landed a job in Dallas with Kellar Hope Foundation, an aid organization that provided families in Third World countries with clothes, shelter, food, and basic education. Not long after moving to Dallas, Mia discovered she was pregnant. The following years were busy with Michael's job and their growing family. Michael never lost the travel bug, however. One day he came home from work and told Mia that there was an opening for a project manager at the office in Sudan.

"Sudan? Isn't that country a war zone?"

"I think Khartoum is safe, Mia. I know Sudan gets a lot of bad press, but the guys in the office say that the city is safer than other parts of the country."

Mia eyed him suspiciously. "What happened to the guy who used to have the job? Maybe he was kidnapped."

Michael threw his head back and laughed. "Come on, Mia, you haven't lost your sense of adventure, have you? Besides, remember how we've always said we want to go and share Jesus' love with those who don't know Him? This is our chance!"

With his killer tan and black hair, Michael would blend in with the people of Sudan. On the other hand, Mia was blonde and fair. She was going to stand out. But Mia couldn't resist Michael's charm, even after years of marriage. And besides that, Michael was right — they had never planned to stay in Dallas forever.

So Mia traded her trendy clothes for ultra-conservative ones. Michael traded his suits for slacks, polo shirts, and a pair of sandals. They packed what they could fit in suitcases and moved to Africa with their three children. Mia's friends back in Texas thought she and Michael were crazy, and she might have agreed—if God hadn't led her to believe this was what He wanted.

Lord, my friends back home don't understand. Sometimes I don't even understand. But I know You want us here. I just don't know why.

Mia's impromptu prayer was interrupted by the loud *Zing!* of the bell at the outer gate. She turned away from the red roses and made her way across the yard, hoping the loud noise hadn't awakened the children from their naps.

When Mia opened the gate, she saw her friend Beth, somehow looking fashionable in her long denim skirt and long-sleeved light-blue t-shirt with a matching scarf. Beth smiled and held up a small, brown bag. Beth worked as a nurse for Kellar Hope Foundation and was the first person to introduce herself to Mia at the office welcome party when she and Michael first arrived. Mia had been encouraged to learn that Beth was a Christian. And because of their mutual desire to share Jesus with people, they quickly became friends.

"Beth, am I glad to see you! My conversations today so far have consisted of, 'Do you need to go potty?' 'Don't stick that in your mouth!' and a few rounds of 'Head, Shoulders, Knees, and Toes.'"

Beth laughed and stepped inside the gate. She was slender and lithe. Her long, dark hair was pulled back into a ponytail, the hairstyle that most of the Western women adopted. It was too hot for women to wear their hair down, and it seemed inappropriate anyway, as most of the Sudanese women covered their heads.

"I brought you a treat!" Beth opened the brown bag to show two containers of gelato ice cream.

Mia took the bag from Beth's hands and gave her a hug. She had to stand on her tiptoes to reach her friend. "Oooh! Peach and chocolate. My favorites."

"I didn't call first because I knew you'd be here," Beth said, following Mia across the yard and into the shade of the veranda.

Only the ice cream kept Mia's emotions from plummeting. *Of course I'd be here. Where would I go?* With three little children to tote around — plus a backpack of diapers, water bottles, baby wipes, snacks, and toys — how many places were worth the trouble?

People like Beth, on the other hand, were seldom home. They could work a fulfilling job, study a new language, make friends, and have a new story every day about their experiences in a foreign land. People like Beth were romantic. She always had a story from the displacement camps. Many of her stories were sad; some were funny. But all of them were a fascinating depiction of the lives of Sudanese people who had been displaced by political unrest, famine, and war.

Beth also volunteered at an orphanage.

"Those little babies are not allowed to be adopted, Mia!" she had said once. "Can you believe it? Even if I wanted to, it is not legal for me to adopt them. I don't know what the future holds for them. No Christian family is allowed to adopt them and no Muslim family would ever be willing to. I hold their tiny, sickly bodies and whisper, 'Jesus loves you, little one.'"

Holding African orphans . . . nursing war victims . . . that was far from Mia's life. Hers was spit-up, dirty dishes, the alphabet song, and occasional forays into the world beyond the cement walls that surrounded her. She tried to cheer herself. *At least I get to eat ice cream.*

The two walked inside and Mia fetched two spoons from the kitchen and motioned for Beth to sit on the sofa. Annie and Dylan were napping. Corey was sitting on his bed playing with Legos. Beth and Mia settled in the living room with the containers of ice cream between them.

"I just don't know what to do," Beth said after swallowing her first bite.

"What do you mean? What's up?"

"It's Nafeesa. You remember, my friend from the camp. You know, she is a devout Muslim, but she really does love me and respects what I have to say. I talk to her about Jesus all the time and remind her that He loves her and her family."

Beth's love for Christ permeated everything she said and did. Yet, somehow, Nafeesa continued to be friends with Beth. Perhaps the woman saw in Beth the peace that she herself longed for.

"Nafeesa has invited me to come to her daughters' circumcision party next week. She's too poor to pay for separate parties for Muna and Raya. I think that's why she waited this long for Muna's procedure. Now they will both be cut on the same day.

Nafeesa tells me the girls won't be able to marry unless she does this. I don't even think she believes it is wrong. But how can I go to this party? Won't it look as if I approve of female circumcision?"

"That's a tough call, Beth." Mia scooped another spoonful and looked out the window. "It's hard to separate culture from religion and moral standards. They seem intertwined here in Sudan, always tripping over each other. Who is going to perform the circumcision?"

"That's the other bad part. Nafeesa can't afford a good midwife. She's just going to hire a woman from the neighborhood, and I've heard terrible stories about her."

Mia grimaced and decided not to ask for any details. Instead, she said, "Isn't female circumcision illegal here in Khartoum?"

"Officially, yes. In practice, though, most Muslim girls have some degree of circumcision performed on them. Traditionally, Sudanese men won't marry a girl who is uncircumcised. They believe that a girl will stay pure if she is cut and sewn so that promiscuity is impossible, or at least very painful."

Against her will, Mia visualized what such a procedure might look like. "Isn't it dangerous?"

"Yes." Beth's voice suddenly went into nurse mode. "The reality is that many health problems can result from this procedure, both while the girls are young as well as later in marriage and childbirth. In the case of Nafeesa's daughters, the risk is even higher. I'm certain that the so-called midwife will not use a clean instrument. I also know how dirty Nafeesa's house is. How can she help it? She is living in a displacement camp. The chance of infection will be high."

"Well, if you attend the party, I think Nafeesa will feel like you approve. But if you don't go, that could offend her."

"I know," Beth said, her brows creased.

They had polished off the rest of the dessert in silence by the time Annie walked out from her bedroom, a hopeful grin on her face. Her blonde curls bounced as she walked. She looked like a miniature version of her mother. Mia checked her wristwatch. Yes, nap time was over and with it, the ability to have a serious conversation with her friend.

Six-year-old Corey followed behind Annie with a Lego creation to show Beth. He was dark-headed like Michael.

"Auntie Beth, look what I made! It's a rocket that shoots missiles from the front and the back!" He held his creation with one hand, pointing out its features with the other.

Mia could hear Dylan jabbering to himself in his bed. Three-ring circus: now open for business.

❖ CHAPTER 2 ❖

Chopped onions danced in the frying pan and the rich aroma filled the sweltering kitchen. Mia opened a can of tomato paste and then scoured her collection of little jars looking for spices to flavor a homemade pasta sauce. The ring of the telephone in the living room broke her concentration.

Truthfully, she was as pleased to leave the kitchen as a child going to recess. Sweat glided down her back and her shoulder-length ponytail pasted itself to the back of her neck. She needed a break from the heat. As she ran to pick up the phone, she passed Dylan. He toddled toward the kitchen, clearly on an exploration mission. At two years old, Dylan got into just about anything his chubby little hands could reach. With his curly blonde hair and blue eyes, he was a cutie, but that was a decoy to distract Mia from his mischievous streak.

As she picked up the receiver, Mia thought about the knife sitting on the kitchen counter. *I don't think he can reach it.* Then she remembered the onions sautéing on the stove. *Yikes, better make this quick.*

It was Beth. "The circumcision party for Nafeesa's daughters is postponed for three weeks. Nafeesa doesn't have enough money yet. I know she is hoping that I will help financially, but I just can't, Mia."

"Yes, it's better not to." Mia eyed the door of the kitchen.

"I've decided not to attend the party," Beth said. "Instead, I'm going to visit the family beforehand and then maybe the next day, you know, to check on the girls."

Beth sounds tired. Probably weary of thinking about how to handle this. Sudanese people had many traditions that perplexed Mia. But female circumcision went beyond that. She didn't know how the practice could be justified in anyone's tradition.

"It sounds like you've chosen a good compromise. I will be praying for the girls and also for you. Beth, I'm sorry, but Dylan is on the loose and I think I better catch him."

"Oh, all right, I understand. See you tomorrow."

Mia quickly hung up the phone and dashed toward the kitchen, but as she did, Dylan emerged, proudly holding up a plastic bowl for Mia to see. "Mommy!"

"Oh, what a sweet boy, of course you can play with that." Mia smiled and watched the back of her young son as he headed off to his bedroom, probably to put some toys into the bowl. Upon entering the kitchen, Mia's foot splashed in a puddle of water . . . then she saw that the puddle stretched all the way across the kitchen. Dylan had turned on the faucet to the container of filtered water and walked away. All the drinking water had drained onto the kitchen floor and the container was now empty.

She remembered the onions, now beginning to char. She sloshed through the water to turn off the stove. *No use crying over spilt drinking water,* she mused, proud of herself for remaining calm. She dumped a bucket of tap water into the filtering system, hoping it would filter fast enough to have water to drink with dinner. Next, she took the mop and coaxed all the water off the floor, then rung it out on the small back porch off the kitchen.

Mia decided to check on Dylan before starting anything else. He was just leaving the bathroom, where he had removed his disposable diaper and stuffed it into the toilet. When Mia arrived, the diaper had already soaked up the toilet water and ballooned into a giant stopper. Mia sighed and stuck her hand in the toilet, firmly gripped the diaper, and tugged. It made a squishy sound and then a loud slurp, like a giant suction cup. Finally, it released its hold. Screwing up her face in disgust, she dumped the enormous drippy glob into the plastic-lined trash basket. She removed the plastic bag and lugged the contents to the trash barrel outside.

When Mia returned, Dylan was sitting on the living room floor. He had filled the plastic bowl with crayons. His plump hand held the red one and he was studiously scribbling long strokes on the white tile floor.

Mia stopped and took a breath, looking at the ceiling. *Someone get me off this train!*

The phone rang again. Mia found herself imagining it was Michael calling to say he would take the family out for dinner. It didn't matter that there were only a handful of restaurants to choose from. Mia did not want to eat spaghetti with a sauce made from tomato paste and charred onions. *If ever there was a day for Prince Charming to sweep me off my feet, this is it!*

"Hello?"

"Hi, hon."

Mia smiled. "Hi, dear! Are you about to leave the office?"

"I need to work late, Mia. I won't be home for dinner. Reports are due tomorrow and I just got the information today. It's going to be a late night."

"Oh." Mia's voice wilted. "All right then, I'll save you some spaghetti."

"I'll be home as soon as I can." Michael's voice was strained.

"All right ..." She hated to make him feel guilty, but she couldn't hide the sadness in her voice. Sure, the job was important. But so was family. Hadn't he already worked late several nights this week?

The following day was Friday and Corey's seventh birthday. Fridays in Khartoum were not work days. At noon, every devout Muslim man, and even the not-so-devout, went to the local mosque to hear the Friday sermon and to pray. After the midday service, most Muslim families spent the afternoon and evenings together. The government required that offices and schools be closed on Fridays so Michael didn't go to work and Corey didn't go to school.

To celebrate Corey's birthday, Mia invited Beth for lunch. She planned to take cupcakes to Corey's class at school but as far as a party at home, well, Corey didn't have any friends in the neighborhood and besides that, Mia didn't have the energy to throw a party. She decided to keep it simple and hoped Corey wouldn't mind.

After lunch, Mia filled a large plastic kiddie pool with water and the adults sat under the shade of the veranda while the kids splashed in the water.

Michael and Beth traded stories about projects in the displacement camps and challenges at the office. Mia listened quietly. She tried to squelch the pesky jealous feelings that cropped up when Beth and Michael talked. They were professionals and had so much in common. She missed having adult conversation on topics other than children.

When compared with the work that Michael and Beth did, her work didn't seem very important. They were improving the quality of life for poor Sudanese people. What could be nobler than that?

Mia looked at her children, laughing and playing. Raising these children was noble. But why was she so frustrated about it?

Beth sipped the last of her limeade. "This is delicious, Mia. Is it homemade?"

"Yes. Straight from the limes on our tree," Mia said. "We get so many that I hardly know what to do with them all."

"I'll take some, then I can make some of this at home. It's so refreshing that I've almost forgotten how hot it is out here."

"Let's go get you some now." Mia stood and set her own cup

on the plastic table. The women headed across the yard to collect the limes that had ripened and fallen off the tree. The ground was dotted with the dark green fruit.

Mia watched Beth out of the corner of her eye as they worked. Beth appeared to have it together. She was confident and spoke Arabic well. She knew her neighbors and conversed knowledgeably about Sudanese culture.

"Beth, I can't figure out how to meet Sudanese women in my neighborhood." Mia paused, embarrassed to admit her problem to someone who seemed to have assimilated so well. "I take walks with the kids, but I don't ever see women out and about. How am I supposed to interact with them?" The familiar frustration flooded her heart again and she let her feelings flow out in words. "If I can't meet the Sudanese people around me, I can't build friendships, and I will dry up like a dying leaf. If that is the case, I might as well go back to Texas. What good am I doing here?"

Beth grabbed a lime from the ground then stood up and looked at Mia. "You are pretty upset about this, aren't you?"

Mia nodded.

"OK, tell me what you want. What's your goal?"

"I want to meet people, to help people, to love people with the heart of Jesus. But I don't know how to do that if I never meet people. Sometimes I feel absolutely imprisoned behind these cement walls." Mia flung her arms out to her sides, as though introducing her cement wardens.

Beth kept her gaze on Mia, ignoring the introduction. Then she bent over and began picking up more limes, filling the patch pockets of her skirt until they bulged.

"For Sudanese women, much of life takes place within the confines of the outer walls. You can't meet women out on the street. You have to get behind their walls. You know, for all the bad press that the Sudanese get for being anti-American, the average Sudanese person is really quite friendly and hospitable.

Besides, the women don't care about all the politics. They are just concerned with daily life."

Mia knew that for a woman, life in Khartoum revolved around her social visits. For a Muslim woman, there were only a handful of events that permitted her to leave her home: weddings, funerals, births, religious holidays, praying at the mosque, and visiting relatives or friends. Occasionally, a woman could go to the market, provided she did not go alone.

"But how can I get behind their walls?"

Beth slowly straightened up again. Her pockets were filled to capacity and her hands held several limes. "Well ..." She looked at the tops of the cement walls, as if the answer to Mia's predicament was perched atop the barriers like a stray cat. "Let's see. I can tell you have a neighbor with young children because I can hear them. Listen!" She pointed to the wall on the right.

Sure enough, even over the noise of the children playing in the pool, Mia could hear the voices of a young child, and maybe a teenager, as well as a mom coming from the house next door. Mia and Beth closed their eyes and listened. Then Beth dropped the limes in her right hand and grabbed Mia's hand.

"Oh, Lord," she prayed, "we know that You have put Mia and her family right in this very house for a reason. Children are a great bridge between us and our Muslim neighbors and we know that Mia has neighbors with children. We pray that you would show her how to meet them, and we pray that she would have a great influence for Christ, even from her own home."

❖ CHAPTER 3 ❖

*M*ichael worked on Saturdays. Mia regretted that he only had Friday off each week, but at least they got to have a quiet cup of coffee together on Saturdays before the children woke up and the day began. Mia sat across from him at the dining table, watching him eat the eggs she'd just scrambled.

"Sorry there's no bacon for you today."

Michael chuckled. "When Khartoum stores sell bacon, well, that will be the end of times."

Mia smiled. "So what's going on at work today?" She stirred a second spoon of powder creamer into a steamy mug of coffee.

"Well, the reports didn't get sent in to the office in Dallas in time because some of the documents from the displacement camps haven't been filled out yet. Everyone at the office is pretty stressed."

"That sounds like fun."

"Yea, a blast." Michael popped the last bit of eggs into his mouth and chewed thoughtfully. "It's not that bad though. The reports will eventually get done. It just takes a lot of energy and some late nights."

Michael wiped his mouth with a napkin, pushed his chair back, and stood.

"Time to go, huh?" Mia stood as well.

"Yep, can't be late." He grabbed his briefcase and walked toward the door. Then he stopped and turned around. His sudden move startled her. But when he took her in his arms, she relaxed. "I love you, Mia. You are a doing a great job here, honey. I know it's not easy."

"Thanks, Michael," Mia whispered into his shoulder. Enveloped in his arms, Mia forgot about the struggles of motherhood and loneliness and the cement enclosure she lived in. She was just Mia, the real Mia, and he was Michael, the man with seven roses who loved her on the continent of Africa as tenderly as he had on the continent of America.

Mia watched Annie stack blocks into a tall tower later that morning. She grinned. Annie often played with dolls, but she also liked to play with her brothers' toys.

"Today we are going to meet our neighbors," Mia said. The statement was more to convince herself rather than inform the kids. After Beth's prayer the day before, Mia determined she would meet the owners of the voices they had heard over the wall.

"I want to watch a movie, Mommy," Annie said. Her tower toppled over and she eyed the destruction with disapproval. She gathered the blocks that were within her reach and began to stack them again. The noise of the falling blocks yanked Dylan's attention away from the board book he was perusing. He threw the book behind him as he headed toward Annie's building project.

"Dylan," Mia said firmly, "how do we treat books?"

Dylan stopped and looked at her, then at the book lying open on the floor, and then back at her again. Mia waited. *Please just pick up the book, Dylan.* Her expression remained firm. Dylan appeared to be weighing the pros and cons of disobeying her.

Then his face brightened and he said, "Uh-oh, Mommy!" He retrieved the book from the floor and set it carefully on the bookshelf before turning and giving Mia a prize-winning smile.

"That's a good boy, Dylan. Now come on, kids, we are getting dressed and going to visit our neighbors. You need to wear shirts, boys."

"It's hot, Mom!" Corey said while lying on his bed reading a comic book.

"Do I have to wear shoes?" Annie asked.

"Yes, shoes and shirts for everyone. Now hurry, before Mommy loses her nerve."

"What's a nerve?" Annie asked.

"It's what Mommy needs in order to go next door. Now, Corey, make sure your brother finds his sandals. I'm going to change my clothes and get ready to go."

Luckily, for Mia, she had remembered the night before that she had a loaf of banana bread in the freezer. *That will be a kind gesture and an excuse to show up next door.* Mia went to the kitchen to place the thawed loaf on a glass plate and covered the whole thing with clear plastic wrap. Then she went to her bedroom and selected a long-sleeved red blouse to wear with her long denim skirt. She found her black scarf with red roses to wear around her neck. Unsure how strict her neighbors were, she wanted to be prepared to cover her hair if necessary.

Children in tow and banana bread in hand, Mia was at least physically ready to meet her neighbors. But as she herded her little ones across the yard and through the front gate, her stomach seized into a tight ball. This was crazy. What was she doing? She didn't even speak Arabic very well. What if they didn't speak English? What if showing up at their front door without an invitation was a cultural taboo?

"Are you all right, Mom?" Corey was looking up at her with a quizzical expression. "Your face looks funny."

"I'm OK, Corey." Mia looked down at her son. Then she stopped, right in front of the gate to their house. "Actually, Corey, I'm nervous. I don't know if this is a good idea or not."

Corey grinned. "It's a great idea." He looked up and down the street before he continued in a whisper, "We get to share Jesus' love. Like you said we should."

Mia smiled. "Yes, you're right Corey. OK, let's go."

As Mia shut the gate, she squeezed her eyes closed for just a moment and whispered a prayer for courage. The sidewalk, or what used to be one, was more jumbled cement chunks than an actual walking path. The foursome picked their way carefully to the house next door. The cement walls were high and Mia could only see the tops of a lime tree and a bougainvillea peering at her over the enclosure. She didn't hear any voices on the other side.

Maybe they'll be gone, she thought. *"Well, I tried, but they weren't home,"* she imagined telling Beth, with a shrug.

"You'll just have to keep trying until you meet them," replied the imaginary Beth.

Ugh! Better just do it now and get it over with. She paused in front of the metal gate, but Corey moved past her and, standing on tiptoe, rang the doorbell.

A loud ring, like a school bell, sounded and Corey laughed.

"That was loud!" he said, and reached up to ring it again.

"No, Corey!" Mia grabbed his hand. "Once is enough."

Mia heard footsteps approach the gate, then she heard the rattle of a slide-lock opening. The gate cracked open and a teenage boy peered out. He was skinny with a shock of black hair and dark piercing eyes. His sharp facial features were Arab while his dark skin and kinky hair hinted to intermarriage with Africans somewhere in his lineage. Mia had learned that most Arabs in Sudan had mixed features like this boy.

"Salaam aleykum!" Mia greeted him, "Peace be upon you!"

"Aleykum wassalaam," he returned. "And on you peace." He opened the gate wider and with a swoop of his hand invited Mia and her children in.

Just like that, she was inside the walls of a Sudanese Arab home. Why had she thought it would be more difficult?

The house was similar to Mia's, with a yard in front and two cement steps leading up to a veranda. A heavyset woman sat in a chair just outside the front door. She stood when she saw the guests walking toward her.

She wore a shapeless blue housedress with geometric designs embroidered in bright green and orange along the hem and neckline. Mia imagined that she probably wore a *tobe* over her dress when she went outside. The woman wore a scarf stretched tightly around her face so that no hair showed. It looked uncomfortable. Mia wondered if she had to cover her hair any time someone rang the doorbell or if she kept it covered all the time. She spoke in Arabic to the teenage boy, who promptly fetched plastic chairs from the far side of the veranda and arranged them beside the woman's chair.

"*Utfuduli! Utfuduli!*" the woman said, pointing at the chairs, "Please, sit down!"

Mia and Corey sat. Annie and Dylan stood on either side of Mia, leaning against her lap. Mia smiled. *Now what? I had not thought past getting through the gate.* Then she remembered the banana bread in her hands.

"This is for you!" she said in Arabic, using a phrase she had been practicing. She held out the glass plate. "It is bread with banana in it. I am your neighbor from next door." *Duh, Mia, as if she doesn't know. I'm sure everyone on the street knows that a* khawadja *(foreigner) family lives in that house.*

"*Shukran! Shukran!*" the woman exclaimed as she took the plate, "Thank you!" She said something quickly to the teenage boy, who nodded and went into the house. He emerged with a younger boy who looked to be the age of Corey. He was skinny with dark hair and striking eyes just like the teenager.

"Come inside and play with my brother, Saleh," said the older of the two. His English was smooth and steady, though he had a strong accent. Corey looked at Mia and she nodded and smiled at him.

"Yes, Corey, you can go play."

"Me too!" squeeled Dylan. Mia nodded.

She looked down at Annie. "Do you want to go, too?"

Annie nodded eagerly and her blonde curls bounced. Mia let her follow the boys into the house, but a part of her worried. Should she let her little girl go into the house with the boys? She was still very young. Would Corey keep an eye on her? Was it wise to let her daughter out of her sight with these strangers? *Lord, please protect Annie.*

Mia tried to push her worries aside by turning to her hostess. "My name is Mia," she said in Arabic.

"I am Hanaan."

"Have you lived here long?" asked Mia.

"We have lived in this house five years. We lived in Dubai, but we decided to move back to raise our children in our home country. What do you think of Khartoum? It is a very dirty place, is it not?"

"Khartoum is OK," Mia answered, pleased with herself for understanding the Arabic that Hanaan spoke. "The important thing is the people; I like the people."

"*Masha' Allah!*" Hanaan said, "Praise be to Allah!"

It seemed to Mia that every Muslim in Khartoum said *Masha' Allah* to just about anything. Everything deserved a hearty Masha' Allah: good food, newborn babies, health, money, and compliments.

"But there is one problem," Mia said. "I have a hard time meeting women. I don't know a good place to meet them." What was she doing? Why was she confiding in a stranger? Mia felt compelled to say this to Hanaan even when her mind told her it was crazy to confide in a Muslim. What if Hanaan asked her why she wanted to meet women? Her whole reason was to share with them about Jesus. As a Muslim, Hanaan would certainly not approve of her intentions.

"*Masha' Allah,* you want to meet women in Sudan? You are a good person, Mia. I can see that. I am going to a *subhia* for the fiancée of my husband's colleague. It is next week. You should come with me. You can meet women there."

Mia's eyes widened. "Really?" she asked, "I can come?"

"Yes, you must," Hanaan said. "The bridal dance is Sudanese culture. You must attend a *subhia* if you want to know about Sudanese women. Now please, relax."

The Arab woman stood and carried Mia's plate of banana bread into the house, leaving Mia alone on the veranda. She strained to hear what was happening inside. She heard laughing and scattered words of both English and Arabic and the slap of children's feet running on the cement floors. The children did not need language to communicate. Children's play translated into any language.

A few minutes later Hanaan's figure filled the doorway. She was holding a silver tray and on the tray were glasses of an orange-colored drink. Her teenage son followed her onto the veranda with a tray of cookies and candies.

"Come children, we shall eat," she called, as she set the tray on a table. "Aladiin, put the cookies here," she pointed to the table, "and tell Saleh to come." Hanaan fussed over the children like a mother hen, making sure each one had enough to eat and drink. Mia was able to relax now that Annie was in her sight. Would she ever feel comfortable sending Annie here to play without accompanying her? She decided that the best thing to do would be to come with them when the children wanted to play. Besides, it would give her a chance to practice speaking some Arabic with Hanaan.

Shortly after the children had returned indoors to continue playing, Hanaan turned to Mia and said, "Eight o'clock next Friday."

"What?" Mia was confused.

"On Friday night at eight o'clock, we are going to the *subhia*."

"Oh, yes, of course. Shall my husband come too?"

Hanaan gasped and searched Mia's eyes as if trying to discern something.

"Or . . . I could just come alone," Mia said sheepishly. What had she said wrong?

Hanaan's shocked expression melted into a warm smile. "You have never been to a *subhia?*" she asked. When Mia shook her head, Hanaan gave a low chuckle. "I will meet you at eight o'clock on Friday, but only you, Mia. You will see why."

❖ CHAPTER 4 ❖

Samia and Halimah sat together near the back of a decrepit bus. With every bump, a loose spring in the seat cushion jabbed Halimah's thigh. At least they were near the back, where the men getting on and off the bus could not hassle them. The two young Arab students rode together every day; it was safer that way. It was considered shameful for an Arab girl to travel alone.

Halimah tugged on the edge of the sliding window, trying to open it for some fresh air.

"He called me," Samia said quietly, glancing around to make certain that no one on the bus could hear her.

"Who called you?" Halimah asked.

"You know. Nadr!"

"Oh . . ." Halimah stopped struggling with the window and turned to her childhood friend, "What did he say?"

"Well, he didn't talk to me. He talked to Father. He said he is ready to marry me. They talked for a long time, and it seemed like Father was pretty happy in the end. He hasn't mentioned it to me though."

"Why hasn't he talked to you? A girl should have a right to decide things about her marriage, about her life! You should talk to your father about this, Samia, really."

Halimah and Samia had been friends since elementary school when Samia's family moved to Khartoum from El Obeid. In high school, Samia was boy crazy and spent much of her time dreaming about boys and secretly meeting with them. Halimah was more of a studious girl than a boy-chaser. She had a solid understanding of her own father's expectations. While she might stomp her feet about women's rights and individualism, Halimah aimed to please her father by graduating in May with an accounting degree and joining the family business. Different as they were, the girls had remained best friends.

When Samia began university, her father arranged for her marriage. She was quite a catch for a Sudanese Arab man. Her skin was light and her eyes dark brown. Her hair, the honor of a Muslim girl, was long and wavy. She pulled her black locks into a ponytail and always carefully covered it with a stylish scarf. She was curvy in all the right places and caught the eye of a number of men. Nadr, however, had first choice because he was her closest cousin of marriageable age. He took a fancy to her and had been saving up for the wedding.

Samia agreed with the arrangement, but she worried about one thing. Samia had a secret. Only she and Halimah knew about it. Well, she and Halimah, and that other boy.

"I can't talk to my father, Halimah, you know that. There's no 'talking' to my father about anything. Whatever he says is what we do. Besides, Nadr is a good choice for me, and it's time I get married." With her last words, her voice trembled. She stared down at the fringes of her headscarf that hung in her lap.

"When does Nadr want to get married?" Halimah asked. That was the whole problem really. It wasn't about the choice of husband or the decision of marriage. It was about the wedding night. That's when everyone would know.

"I can't be sure," Samia replied, "but I heard Father say it would be good to have it after *Eid al-Adha*."

"After *Eid al-Adha!*" Halimah exclaimed. Samia glared at her and Halimah lowered her voice. "Right after *Eid al-Adha?* That's only a few months from now. If they find out, you'll be divorced before you've been a married woman for a day!"

"You think I don't know that?" Samia snapped. "But they aren't going to find out because I have a plan. But I need your help."

The bus creaked to a halt in front of the university. Secrets would have to wait for another time. Halimah hoped Samia wasn't planning to do anything rash. She looked her friend in the eye, begging her to say something that would set her mind at ease, but Samia was done talking. She grabbed her bag off the floor and jumped out of the bus. Halimah followed.

Halimah knew why Mahmoud had created the graduation committee. He was flirtatious and funny and he loved girls. What better way to hang out with girls at university than calling a committee meeting? It was a brilliant idea, really. All the fathers believed it, even Halimah's. So, every week, the graduation committee met in the shade of a large neem tree on the far side of the campus.

Halimah and Samia arrived at the tree and found Jamal reclined against its thick trunk, puffing on a cigarette. Mahmoud held a notebook that belonged to the beautiful 'Isra. He ran in circles laughing while she chased him. Howeida, the quiet one of the group, immediately walked toward the two new arrivals.

"Look what my fiancé sent me this time!" she said, proudly holding out a smart phone.

"Wow," Samia said, touching the phone with her fingertip. "That must have been expensive. Is your fiancé Sudanese?"

"Yes," Howeida replied, "but he lives in Dubai. He works for an oil company. He plans to return to Khartoum to marry me after I graduate."

"But in the meantime," Halimah said, "you get some pretty awesome gifts!"

Howeida giggled. "Yes, it's true. Go ahead, you can hold it! You can't get these here in Khartoum you know, because of the sanctions."

"You can't get anything in Khartoum," Halimah grumbled.

"Well, we are in a war," Jamal said, between puffs of smoke.

"Yes, but my father says there will soon be a peace agreement," Howeida said.

Jamal shrugged and said, "Tell that to the folks in Darfur and see if they believe you."

"Watch how you talk, Jamal," scolded Samia. She looked toward the buildings where students and faculty walked about like busy ants in an anthill. "You may fancy yourself a free-thinker, but this campus has ears."

Halimah wondered what Jamal meant by his comment about Darfur, and why Samia was worried about the campus sprouting ears. Admittedly, she didn't know much about politics. She hardly thought about it, unless she overheard her father and Abdu talking with their guests late in the evenings or on Friday afternoons when they gathered to smoke and drink tea.

She had heard of fighting in the South with those tribes that had strange religions. She knew fighting often erupted in the West against the Fur, those Muslim tribes who rebelled against the government. But in Khartoum, buildings were going up, new businesses were opening, and universities were thriving.

"*Tayib!*" Halimah said, after admiring the phone, "It's time to do some planning for the graduation. My mother is asking what we have been doing and I need to tell her something."

"Yes! Mine too!" 'Isra said. She had retrieved her notebook and returned to the shade of the tree. "I was thinking we could price invitations at a few places."

"Great idea, 'Isra. You live close to Souq alArabi, why don't you get some estimates from there and Jamal could get some quotes from Bahri." They paused and looked at Jamal. He had finished his cigarette and drifted off to sleep.

"He's useless," Halimah muttered.

"All men are useless," 'Isra said. "They are just good for giving us money and the rest of the time they give us pain!"

"Oh yeah?" Mahmoud said, coming up from behind and grabbing 'Isra's notebook again. He took off running across the dusty patches of grass.

"He can have it," 'Isra said and shrugged. "It will only make him jealous when he sees the notes to Omar that I wrote inside!"

The day's classes were tedious and to top it off, the electricity had been out so that even the lecture rooms with ceiling fans had morphed into blazing furnaces. Sitting next to Samia on the bus ride home, Halimah could smell her own body odor, even though she'd applied perfume to her armpits several times throughout the day. *I just need a bath, that's all there is to it. I'll take one as soon as I get home.* But first things first. Halimah was going to squeeze some information out of her friend.

"What are you going to do? And what do you need from me?" Halimah said quietly, leaning toward Samia.

"I'm going to hire Nur Hamid." Samia mouthed the name, not even daring to say it out loud.

"Are you crazy? She is a Southerner. Not only could she give you some disease, she'll blab your story all over the city."

"No, she won't tell," Samia replied. "That's why she costs a lot of money. I'll pay her to be quiet. I'm not the only one who's ever had this problem you know. She'll cut me again and then sew me back up so that it looks like the circumcision I had as a little girl was never messed up. It will be as if I'm a virgin again. They say she is very skilled. She can make my past go away."

Halimah doubted that the woman was skilled enough to cut the guilt from Samia's heart, but she remained silent while her friend continued to speak.

"I just need to have a month to recover. That's where you come in. I cannot go home to recover. My mother will know as soon as I walk in the door. I need to stay with you."

"For a month?" Halimah asked. "You know you are always welcome in my house, but your mother has never let you stay away for more than one night."

"Maybe just a couple of weeks. We'll say you are helping me with the wedding."

"Well, that's believable," Halimah replied, "especially if the wedding is to be after *Eid alAdha*. It definitely won't be a lie. You have a lot of planning to do. Where are you going to get the money to hire Nur Hamid?" She silently mouthed the name, just like Samia had done.

"I've saved some already, and I'll ask my dad for my money for *Eid al-Fitr* early," she answered.

"Well, that's pretty confident, coming from the Samia who can't even ask her father what he said to her fiancé on the phone!" Halimah jested. Samia slapped her friend hard on the leg with her psychology textbook, but grinned as she did it.

When the bus approached Halimah's neighborhood, she snapped her fingers and the bus driver pulled over. The girls said goodbye and Halimah walked down a wide dirt road toward her house.

The ten-minute walk gave her time to ponder Samia's predicament. *It's not like she has an alternative.* In high school, Samia slept with a boy and messed up her childhood circumcision. The boy moved away soon after the incident and she never saw him again. She confided in Halimah about a year later, when she could not bear the guilt or fear alone any longer. Together the girls kept Samia's secret. As long as she was not married, no one had to know. But—if anyone found out—she could be disowned or even stoned to death.

Halimah cringed to think of the pain that Samia would have to go through to keep her secret hidden and spare her own life. Nur Hamid was a legend among the university girls. No one that Halimah knew had ever been to her, or even knew for certain that she was for real. She was said to be an old woman from a Southern tribe who was as black as charcoal and as wrinkly as an elephant. A girl could hire her to reconstruct a childhood circumcision to look like she was still a virgin. Halimah did not have to experience such excruciating pain because she had never slept with a man. And her own circumcision was not as severe as her friend's. Samia had undergone a pharaonic circumcision. She had been sewn shut with only a tiny hole left for her menstrual flow.

In Sudanese Arab culture, family and neighbors discussed circumcision when the subject of marriage came up. Men wanted to know if a potential bride had been circumcised. Nadr knew what kind of circumcision Samia had, and he would know that she should bleed a lot on her wedding night.

Samia had no choice. She had to go to Nur Hamid. *I just hope that old woman can do a good job. Samia will have to pay enough money to keep Nur Hamid quiet. Her life depends on it.*

❖ CHAPTER 5 ❖

*H*alimah set her book bag just inside the front door and followed the sounds of clanking pots to the kitchen. She paused in the doorway and watched her mother move about busily. She was tall and plump, like a good Sudanese Arab wife should be. Halimah tried to imagine a younger version of Mama. She would still be tall, but her teenage figure would be hidden in the shapeless dresses that she now wore.

Mama married Father when she was a teenager and nine months later bore him a son, Abdu. Over the following years she had three more children. Halimah was the second, then Ali, then Rania. Mama did not finish high school, and she was proud of Halimah for attending university. She kept herself busy at home: cooking, cleaning, and spreading the latest neighborhood gossip.

"There you are, Halimah." Her mother waved her hand toward the countertop. "Come cut these onions."

Startled out of her reverie, Halimah gathered the four large purple onions waiting for her on the kitchen counter, selected a knife, and sat down at a small wooden table in the middle of the room. She pulled the skins off all four onions and placed them in a bowl of water to keep them from making her eyes water.

"Your cousin Bashir has been saying crazy things again. Last week he called his mother by his sister's name, and . . ." Mama paused and looked at Halimah, lowering her voice. "He has begun to wet the bed."

"Mama," Halimah replied, irritation building in her voice, "he's just under a lot of stress. They need to leave him alone and quit telling him he's crazy!" Halimah finished the first onion and started on the second. The water was helping some, but she was still tearing up. Or were they tears of indignation? *So what if Bashir is acting strange? He is only fourteen; aren't all teenage boys strange?*

"He's demon-possessed, Halimah! It's nothing to trifle about." The older woman shook her head as she started a flame on the kitchen burner and began to fry chunks of lamb, grabbing some of the freshly chopped onions and adding them to the hot oil. She watched the food sizzling for a few seconds. Without raising her eyes from the pan of meat, she said flatly, "They are sending him to a *khalwa* out past Atbara."

"A *khalwa*? What is that going to do for him, Mama? If he has stress or a mental problem, a *khalwa* will not help him." Halimah willed her voice to be calm.

"Yes it will, Halimah," her mother said in a stern tone. She reached over and grabbed the girl's arm harshly, "and don't you say otherwise to your father. It is not your place to disagree." She let go roughly, but her voice returned to normal, "The *sheikh* there knows how to handle these things. He will read the Qur'an to Bashir and make him memorize *suras*, scripture that will help him. The *sheikh* will help him."

The sheikh will beat *him*, is what Halimah wanted to say, but she didn't want Father to hear that she had been impudent. She had no doubt that he would hit her for such behavior. In the past, he had hit her for voicing an opinion that was different from his. Halimah did not want to cross him again. It wasn't that Father didn't love her. Most girls had been hit by their fathers or brothers. The men of the house were the rulers. But not just the men, even Halimah's younger brother Ali could tell her what to do. In the order of things, Ali was above Halimah, because he was male.

Halimah's sleep was fitful. She dreamed about Bashir. She dreamed he was at the *khalwa,* the Islamic school. She dreamed that men chained his legs together at the ankles so he wouldn't run away. She dreamed that the *sheikh* beat him with heavy wooden prayer beads if he couldn't quote the *suras* word for word.

What *suras* would they teach him? Did Halimah even know them? What if Halimah were beaten for not quoting the Qur'an correctly? She should study it more. Her father would swell with pride if she attended classes at the mosque.

Halimah dreamed that she was reading the Qur'an in her bed. She dreamed that she wet the bed and that her father sent her to the *khalwa.* Halimah saw the *sheikh* coming toward her. She tried to run, but he hit her with his wooden beads right across the face. Halimah cried out in pain.

"Halimah? Halimah? Are you OK?" She opened her eyes with a start, saw her sister Rania, and realized she was in bed at home. She breathed a sigh of relief. Rania turned on the lamp by her bed and looked at her big sister with a worried expression.

"Oh . . . Rania . . . yes, I am OK. I had a nightmare I think," Halimah stammered, "Just go back to sleep."

"It's already four-thirty, Halimah. Abdu will be getting up to pray at the mosque."

Halimah groaned and rolled over in bed. Abdu was a good Muslim. He prayed five times a day without fail. When he bowed in prayer, he pressed his forehead so strongly against the prayer rug that he had a *zibeeb,* a dark bruise called a "raisin" that marked his piety. He also followed the other pillars of Islam: giving to the poor, repeating the *shihada,* fasting during Ramadan, and he'd already been on the pilgrimage to Mecca.

Every morning he would put on his white *jallabeeya,* carry his prayer mat, and walk to the neighborhood mosque to pray the sunrise prayer with other faithful Muslims. Abdu prayed even more than his father, who had been known to skip a few prayer times here and there.

Women were not expected to pray at the mosque, but a separate section was provided for them, should they want to. Halimah always prayed at home like her mom, but Abdu wanted her to go to the mosque.

Just as she feared, the door to the girls' bedroom opened and Abdu poked his head in. "It's time to pray, Halimah," he said, then added, "it looks like you are already awake. Come on, get dressed; you can go with me to the mosque."

Halimah groaned again, "I can't, Abdu, I'm on my period!"

"Oh, I see, OK." Abdu awkwardly stepped out of the doorway and the door clicked shut.

"That always works," Halimah said to Rania, grinning. She pulled the sheet over her head and squeezed her eyes shut, "I'm going back to sleep, Rania. Please turn off the light."

Halimah imagined Abdu grabbing his prayer mat and walking to the mosque alone. Halimah wondered if Abdu ever stopped to calculate how often she used that excuse with him. If he did, he would discover that Halimah was supposedly on her period constantly. Lucky for her, he always ended the conversation immediately and never questioned her.

After class later that day, Samia and Halimah rode the bus to the *souq*, the local market, before heading home. In the hustle and bustle of the bus station, Samia whispered into Halimah's ear, "I arranged an appointment to go to Nur Hamid."

"You did? How? When?" Halimah tripped over a stone in the sand-covered bus station and grabbed Samia's arm for support.

"Halimah, you don't need to know the details. It's better if you don't know. Just be ready for me to come to your house on Thursday."

"Thursday. Right." Halimah had not yet talked to Mama about Samia coming. She'd have to do some slick talking when she got home. Maybe she could find a gift for her mother while the girls shopped. She would probably like a new bottle of perfume.

Of all the *souqs*, the one in Omdurman was Halimah's favorite. The Omdurman Souq had shops for anything a person might want. There were shops full of colorful scarves, make-up, gold jewelry, perfumes, dishes, and food. The *souq* was a cacophony of colors, sounds, and smells. The inexperienced shopper might get lost in a *souq* so big. But Halimah knew the place as well as her own neighborhood. Each area sold different items. All the shops were run by men and girls never shopped alone.

Samia and Halimah meandered through the clothes section.

"Look at this shirt, Halimah!" Samia was holding up a tight-fitting, long-sleeved shirt with swirls of pastel flowers.

"It's beautiful but much too small, Samia. Your father will never let you wear that!" Halimah pulled a more sensible blouse off the rack and held it up to her friend. "This one has the same colors."

"That one is ugly," Samia said, her eyes glued to her first choice. "I can cover it with an *abaya* when I am around Father."

"Then you can take off the *abaya* once you leave the house, I know," Halimah replied. She was well aware of Samia's schemes because almost every Sudanese Arab girl did the same thing. Halimah was guilty of using the same tactics with her own father. Even though she thought girls from the Southern tribes were dirty and weird, she couldn't help being a little jealous of them. They were allowed to wear any of the cute clothes sold in the market because they weren't Muslim. "Samia, hurry up and buy that shirt. I want to look at perfume."

They wound through the maze of booths until they came to the make-up and perfume section. Halimah used most of her money to buy a bottle of imported perfume. Mama usually wore the traditional homemade Sudanese perfume. It was brown and watery and smelled like sandalwood, which greatly pleased

Halimah's father. But sometimes she wore store-bought perfume. Her mother would be delighted to have a new bottle. The fresh fragrance would hopefully soften her mood for when Halimah asked if Samia could stay. She would say yes, Halimah was sure, but would she believe their story? Two weeks was a long time.

❖ CHAPTER 6 ❖

"ut why does Samia have to stay for two whole weeks?" Rania asked, her lips formed into a pout.

"Because she and I are working on her wedding plans," Halimah answered impatiently.

"You never talk to me when Samia is here. It's always you and her, talking into the wee hours of the morning and I have to give her my bed too! That's not fair!"

"I'll tell you what," Halimah replied, "You can sleep in my bed with me. You know, like we used to do when you were younger."

Rania thought about that. Now that she was thirteen, she was wearing a scarf to cover her head, and their mother had purchased an *abaya* for her. She was happy to enter the world of womanhood when her period started. But she missed the days when she was just a child. When Rania was younger, she and her big sister would lie side-by-side, whispering quietly late into the night after everyone else had gone to sleep. Halimah would tell her stories, made-up ones about a prince who would come and marry her and take her to a lovely palace that had a beautiful horse just for her, and lots of new clothes. She liked that.

"Fine …" she whined, "she can have my bed."

Halimah had been a young girl, only six years old, when her father's brother, Uncle Asim, got married. The wedding week was full of excitement. Halimah helped her mother and *haboba* cook. They shopped for fancy *tobes*, head-to-toe scarves that married women layered over their clothes. Her *haboba* bought a brand new dress for Halimah. They attended the henna party for Uncle Asim's bride, where she and her closest friends had swirly black flowers and tendrils painted on their hands and feet.

The following night she attended the bridal dance party called the *subhia*, and the *jirtik*, where the bride and groom sat on a red and black wood-framed bed, surrounded by the smoke and pungent smell of *bakhoor,* and spit milk at each other for good luck. Finally, they attended the wedding party where Uncle Asim looked charming and handsome in a brown suit and his bride, Fareeda, looked like a princess. Halimah wanted to be old enough to get married. She wanted to be as beautiful as Fareeda had been.

When all the festivities were over, Uncle Asim and Auntie Fareeda came to *Haboba's* house for their first night together. The following day they would travel to Wad Medani for their honeymoon. Halimah's family also slept at *Haboba's* house. It was a long drive home to Khartoum, and they would not return for a few more days.

Halimah remembered that night, the first night of Uncle Asim's and Auntie Fareeda's marriage. It was late and the newlyweds had gone to bed in their own room but, for some reason, all the women were still awake. They sat in the *hosh*, the garden area, of *Haboba's* large house. They reclined on an assortment of metal beds and chairs that had been dragged out from the mud-brick rooms encircling the dirt yard. They drank hot tea and ate the candy left over from the week of parties. A couple of aunties snoozed on the beds, and *Haboba* told funny stories about a strange new Southern family who had recently moved to her village to get away from the war in Juba.

Halimah leaned over to Mama and whispered, "Why is everyone still awake?"

"*Shh*, child. Just lay down on the bed over there and go to sleep."

Halimah didn't want to go to sleep by herself. She played with the plastic flower arrangements that were used in the wedding. They were pink and purple with plastic green leaves and she imagined that they were the flowers in her own wedding. After what seemed to be a very long time, *Haboba* rose from her chair and walked out of the *hosh*, toward the bedrooms. When she returned, she was smiling brightly.

"Blood is on the cloth," she said proudly.

"*Alhamdullilah!*" chorused the women around the *hosh*. Halimah thought that they seemed to breathe a collective sigh of relief.

"What does that mean, Mama?" Halimah asked.

"It means that Fareeda is a good bride, Halimah," she replied. "She has kept the good name of her family and has brought honor to our family name. If we have nothing else, Halimah, we have honor. You must always guard the honor of our family."

Samia arrived at Halimah's house on the following Thursday. She missed her classes at the university so Halimah knew she had gone to meet Nur Hamid. Samia arrived at four o'clock in the afternoon, just as Halimah and her mother were washing the lunch dishes.

"*Salaam aleykum,*" Samia greeted the women. "Peace to you."

"*Aleykum wassalaam,*" they returned in unison. "And upon you peace."

Samia's acting ability amazed Halimah. Mama did not notice that anything was wrong at all. Had her friend changed her mind about the procedure? Halimah's heart was beating wildly, but she forced herself to calmly, slowly dry the dishes.

"Samia, put your bag down in my room, and I'll meet you there as soon as I finish the dishes with Mama," Halimah said. She hoped her voice sounded natural. Samia obeyed and disappeared from the kitchen door.

"She's probably tired, Mama," Halimah said, answering a question that wasn't asked. "You know, wedding planning can be stressful."

"Well, that will be you soon enough, my dear!" Mama smiled.

Halimah did not want to deal with the subject of her own marriage just then.

"You go take a nap, Mama, I'll put the rest of these dishes away and check on Samia."

Her mother agreed and retired to her own bedroom, leaving Halimah to herself. Halimah preferred it that way. She quickly finished the chore and then found her friend lying on her bed. Her face was pale and sweat trickled down her hairline. Halimah offered her a glass of water and two aspirin.

"So, it's done." Halimah said. It was more of a statement than a question.

"It is," she replied.

Halimah ran her fingers over Samia's hair, then she took her friend's headscarf that had fallen to the floor and used it to wipe the sweat from her brow. *Poor thing,* she thought, *why does the life of a woman feel so much more difficult than the life of a man?* Samia lay on the bed, feverish and sick. Why? To preserve the honor of her family. The words of Mama from many years ago echoed in her head.

Eventually, Samia fell asleep. She was, at least for the moment, relieved of her pain. Halimah peeked into the bag Samia brought. To her surprise, there was nothing in the bag that even resembled wedding plans. *Oh no, Mama will be spying on us for sure, and she'll need to see some evidence of what we're doing.* Halimah looked around her bedroom for notebooks and pencils. She found two pictures of her auntie's wedding, Rania's set of colored pencils, three empty notebooks, and a ballpoint pen. She spread all of her findings on the floor, as if she and her friend had just finished a planning session. She would need to buy some wedding magazines.

Halimah glanced at Samia, still fast asleep. Mama was

napping and Rania would not be home for a few more hours. Halimah tiptoed to the wardrobe that she and Rania shared and opened the wooden doors. Thrusting her arm under the stacks of clothes, she reached to the very back and cautiously retrieved a small black book. She ran her fingers across the leather cover of the *Injil*, a portion of the Christian holy book. Halimah kept it hidden because Abdu and her father would not approve. They would punish her for having an *Injil*, even if it was a holy book.

Halimah closed the wardrobe door and sat on the floor. She leaned against the wardrobe, opened the little book, and looked at its pages. This was not an ordinary book. It was in Arabic and English. This would help Halimah with her English. Halimah flipped to the section called "Romans" and as she did so, she thought about the professor who had given the book to her.

One day a professor at her university gave her the copy of the *Injil* and told her this was the best way to learn English because it had many stories and because the Arabic translation was right beside the English. Halimah grinned. The professor was right, it was easy to pick a small portion to read in English and then compare it to the Arabic on the same page.

Halimah wanted to go back to the university and thank the professor, but she never saw that woman again. Halimah didn't even know her name and she was afraid to ask anyone. What if she was a bad person? Or what if she had been fired? Halimah didn't want to get in trouble for having received a book from her, so she kept the book a secret, even from Samia.

She began to read where she left off the day before in the third chapter. What did it mean that, "now a righteousness from God, apart from law, has been made known, to which the Law and the Prophets testify. This righteousness from God comes through faith in Jesus Christ to all who believe"? She didn't have an answer. She reread the verses in Arabic just to make sure that she understood the English correctly.

In Arabic, she read, "There is no difference, for all have sinned and fall short of the glory of God." *Well, yes, that is true. We have all sinned. But that is why we do good works: to earn our way to heaven, if God wills it. Right?* She continued, "and are justified freely by his grace through the redemption that came by Christ Jesus." Halimah had heard of the prophet Jesus (called *Isa* in Islam), but what was all of this about righteousness by faith in Jesus and justification through redemption by Jesus? Halimah had never heard of these things, but apparently the prophets had testified. Why was she never taught that?

Halimah read for an hour before she heard Samia stir. She shut the *Injil* quickly and returned it to the hiding spot in the wardrobe. She ran to Rania's bed and lay down as if she too had been resting, but her heart was stirred by the words she'd read. *"Therefore, the promise comes by faith, so that it may be by grace and may be guaranteed to all Abraham's offspring." Faith? Grace? Could anything really be guaranteed?* Halimah forced herself to lie still until Samia was fully awake. Then she rose and went to her side.

"How do you feel?" she asked quietly, stroking Samia's hair.

"Sick," she replied, "lots of pain."

"I'll get you some food. You need food, Samia," Halimah's voice was smooth and quiet. Inside, though, her heart melted. She was helpless. She had to do something, anything. Food was all she could come up with. Halimah stood up to go to the kitchen, but Samia weakly grabbed her hand.

"I don't want food, Halimah. Just sit here with me." Halimah sat down on the floor beside the bed. She stroked her friend's hand.

"Samia, you are a hero. What you have done to preserve the honor of your family . . . I can't say that I would . . . well, I just don't know what I would do."

"You would do what I did, Halimah," Samia replied. She closed her eyes and winced, "You would not have a choice."

❖ CHAPTER 7 ❖

$\mathcal{M}$ia listened to the sound of a single *dallooka* drum beat an intoxicating rhythm while an old woman with a nasal voice warbled strange melodies. The audience clapped in time, a few of them singing along. Twinkling party lights glistened like stars against the night sky. A square stage was draped in red cloth and on the stage stood a man, the only man in a sea of women and girls who surrounded the stage.

He looked sharp in his white *jallabeeya*, gold hat, and red sash thrown across one shoulder. In one hand he gripped a long sword. His fingers rubbed nervously against its leather sheath. He began to tap his foot to the beat of the drum, as if trying to pretend he was not the center of attention for 200 women. He really wasn't, not for long anyway.

Within a few moments, a figure draped in shiny red cloth emerged from a nearby tent. This must be the bride. Two women guided the figure—shrouded from head to toe—to the steps of the stage. Once securely on the stage, the figure began to move to the rhythm of the drum.

Slowly, slowly, hands hidden under the folds of cloth unveiled the head to reveal a beautiful face. Eyes were heavily outlined in kohl, lips were cherry red, and black hair fell out of the red scarf and hung all the way down to the waist. Gold dripped from the girl's ears and neck while her hair held a gold-chained headpiece with gold strands cascading down to her shoulders.

As she looked at the man on stage, who must be the groom, the girl began to sway her hips to the beat, while simultaneously untying the floor length scarf from her waist. It dropped to the ground and an older woman on the front row quickly whisked it from the stage. At this point the groom raised his hands and his sword over his head and shook it to the beat of the music, while the audience clapped and cheered. The older women ululated their approval in falsetto tones.

Removing the red scarf had revealed a bride clothed in a satin red sleeveless dress that exposed her shoulders and thighs. Gold bracelets and anklets adorned her arms and legs. Black henna designs swirled like curly vines around her fingers, palms, and arms, and from her toes all the way up to just above her knees. The scent of sandalwood, smoked into her golden skin, drifted into the audience.

Hanaan and Mia sat at a round table close to the stage. Hanaan leaned closely to Mia and spoke loudly, competing with the volume of the performance. "This is the night that the bride will show herself off, not only to her groom, but to his family and all the women of the community. She has been studying these belly dances for six weeks. She has also been doing *dukhaan*."

Mia remembered reading about *dukhaan* in an article on Sudanese weddings. A prospective bride spent several hours a day sitting in a burlap cape over smoldering incense to prepare her skin. She also used lotions and perfumes, oils on her hair, and finally, she'd wax her entire body to remove all her hair except what was on her head. All of this was done to prepare for the wedding. Mia wondered if Esther in the Bible went through similar rituals in her many months of preparation to meet the king.

All around Mia, the women wore beautiful *tobes*, colorful scarves that covered them from head to toe. Even though the *subhia* took place outside under a giant tent, each woman wore dressy high-heeled shoes. Hanaan also wore spikey heels. They stabbed the packed mud when she walked, as if someone had jabbed a pencil into the ground over and over again. Mia glanced down at her own feet. Her flat sandals were dressy but sensible. Sensible did not appear to be an important feature at this function. Mia made a mental note to buy a pair of spikey heels.

As the bride continued her sensual dancing, cheered on by the women who watched, young girls stood as close as they could to the stage. Were they dreaming of the day they would be old enough to do their own bridal dance? Mia remembered dreaming of her own wedding day. Her fantasies were different than these young Arab girls. Back in Texas, as a little girl, Mia dreamed of a white dress with a train of silk and tulle that flowed for yards behind her. She dreamed of pearls and lace, chocolate fountains and a giant strawberry wedding cake.

When Michael and Mia married, Mia's dress didn't have a train. She wore bright red cowboy boots under the billows of silk and tulle. What would these ululating women in their spikey heels think if they knew she had worn boots on her wedding day?

Mia's thoughts were interrupted by Hanaan trying to yell over the beating drum again. "Mia, come with me next week. I will take you to the dervishes in Omdurman."

"What's a dervish?" asked Mia.

"Come with me and you'll find out," Hanaan said.

Mia nodded at Hanaan and tried out her newest phrase, "*Insha' Allah,* if God wills."

"But Michael, Friday is your day off. Why can't you watch the kids? I already told Hanaan I would go with her."

"It's not my fault, Mia. They need someone to go to the displaced camp on Friday. I'm the only one available."

"But you're *not* available, Michael. Your family needs you." Mia hung up the phone. Lately, Michael had been at work so much that most of their conversations took place on the phone.

Mia had never hung up on him before. She'd also never been this mad at him.

He seemed to have energy and time to put into his job but never into his own family. A slow dawning began to surface, a thought Mia had felt but hadn't yet acknowledged. She and Michael were beginning to live parallel lives. Mia made the meals and Michael earned the paycheck. His life was at Kellar Hope and her life was at home. And while their paths crossed occasionally, where did that leave the kids? The raising of the children had been reduced to deciding who was going to babysit them and when.

The phone rang. Mia picked up the receiver but did not say anything. It had to be Michael, and she didn't have anything good to say to him.

"Mia, it's me. I'll ask Beth to go to the camp and I'll watch the kids on Friday."

"Thank you."

Even as she said the words, Mia wondered why she was thanking him. It's not like he was giving up a work day. It was his day off and he should want to be with his kids. She wished she could take back her "thank you" and say "that's more like it," instead.

"Mia, you can't fall apart like this every time something difficult happens."

"What are you talking about?" Mia's voice squeeked as she pretended to be confused, although she knew that Michael was referring to her hanging up on him.

"You have to try to control your emotions, Mia." Michael's voice betrayed his own frustration. "We'll never make it here in Sudan if you don't."

The nerve of that man! Mia hung up the phone on him for the second time. She leaned against the wall and slid down to the floor. She covered her face with her hands and cried.

❖ CHAPTER 8 ❖

*M*ia sat in the back of Hanaan's car. As the driver navigated the empty Friday streets, Hanaan chattered on about her home in Dubai and about how difficult life in Khartoum was.

"There really isn't very much to do here, Mia," she complained. "I take the kids swimming on Fridays, but now they are bored of it. This morning Saleh told me he did not want to go." She threw her hands up in the air, "What am I to do?"

"Will you go back to Dubai?" Mia asked.

"Next year, *insha' Allah*. Just to visit."

I wish I could go back to Texas next year. The truth was, Sudan was not what she thought it would be. Guilt pricked Mia's heart. How could she think that? Michael was doing such a fantastic job at the foundation and had many opportunities to exemplify Jesus. And to top it off, she had prayed for a chance to meet some Arab women, and in the past week she had been invited to two events by Hanaan.

Well, this hardly counts since you haven't shared Jesus with her. You can't even speak Arabic very well.

She should be able to speak Arabic better by now. Michael seemed to catch on quickly. Plus, he had every day in the office that he could "be Jesus" to all the people around him. Mia was finally getting some opportunities of her own, but she hadn't said anything deep yet. She had envisioned that sharing Jesus would be easy. How was she supposed to bring up the subject? Seriously, maybe she should talk to Michael about going home.

"Mia?" Hanaan called her back to the present. "Mia, did you hear me? We are almost at the dervishes. Most Muslims in Sudan are Sunni, you know, but there are also many Sufis. The dervishes are Sufi holy men. The whirling dervishes are performed each Friday before evening prayers at this Sufi mosque. See? Here is the graveyard and back there is the mosque."

The dusty earth was packed down by thousands of pairs of feet that trod the ground of the Omdurman cemetery. Hanaan and Mia stepped out of the car and walked toward the mosque. Mia looked across a sea of brown skin and colorful clothes. The two women walked across a large open area, picking their way through stools made of wire and plastic string where people sat to drink tea out of tiny glass cups. Tea ladies worked their makeshift stations, using little charcoal stoves and jars of tea leaves and spices to make dirty cups of syrupy sweet tea for patrons.

On the other side of the horde of people was the mosque. The square building was the same color as the dusty ground that surrounded it. Green flags on heavy poles stood guard at its entrance. They flapped in the wind, their bright color a stark contrast to the brown surroundings.

Hanaan ushered Mia to the front of the crowd, which was forming into a circle as the sun lowered in the sky. Suddenly, Mia noticed the flags in front of the mosque began to move. They bobbed up and down as they continued to flap in the breeze. Startled at first, Mia watched, and an eerie feeling in her gut made her stomach sink. Then she realized that men had come out of the mosque and picked up the flag poles. That is why they appeared to float toward the crowd. People in the crowd began to chant something that was unintelligible to Mia. A giant, hollow sounding drumbeat began to thump.

Two men, wearing old red and green *jallabeeyas*, walked into the little empty area in the middle of the crowd. They widened the arena by waving the crowd back. Mia and the others moved back against the people behind them; a tight human wall of sweaty bodies. Mia did not want to be in the front, even if Hanaan was proud of herself for finding such a prized spot. Backing up little by little, Mia managed to put a few people between her and the two men.

The chanting continued and then the green flags approached. The crowd parted to let the men with the flags through to the center. Everyone was clapping and chanting. Finally, Mia began to hear the words and understand the chant.

"*La illah 'ila Allah*," over and over again, "There is no god but Allah." The rhythm was catchy and, against her will, Mia found herself repeating the phrase in her head. People all around her smiled and children clapped to the beat. When the flags arrived, so did a large group of men and boys wearing colorful *jallabeeyas*: red, purple, blue, but mostly green. Green was the color associated with Sufi Islam.

More men exited the mosque and joined the dusty human ring. They clapped and chanted and danced to the beat. Some began to spin in circles. Each man that appeared seemed to be stranger than the one before him, his eyes more empty, his hair more messy.

A commotion among the group arose and, as they spread out, Mia saw what must have been the most honored of the dervishes. The man's head was covered with grayish black dreadlocks that looked like they never had been washed. His tangled beard and mustache twisted around his face. He wore a green *jallabeeya* with so many strands of giant wooden beads around his neck that he could hardly turn his head. His hands held an assortment of dirty talismans and amulets.

He is a demon. Mia shuddered. She reconsidered when she saw that what he really looked like was a helpless human controlled by something more powerful than himself. He walked into the center of the dusty ring and around him all the dervishes began to dance. The drum beat went on and on; the chant grew louder and louder.

"*La illah 'ila Allah. La illah 'ila Allah.*"

Three men in green *jallabeeyas*, who Mia guessed were dervishes, began to twirl and twirl, working themselves into a frenzy. Sometimes they would lose their balance and fall to the ground, only to get back up and continue twirling. A teenager began to bite his arm as he twirled. Another dervish went to the front row of the crowd and took a baby from a woman in the crowd. Mia thought that it must have been his baby, or at least some relative's, because the young toddler was wearing a tiny green *jallabeeya* just like his. The dervish held the child and continued to dance to the steady beat and the repetitious chant of the crowd.

An eerie and evil spiritual presence was palpable. Mia felt her skin crawl. She wanted to run away, but she stood frozen, not wanting to attract attention. She watched in horrified fascination as the dervishes, and some of the crowd who joined them in the arena, worked themselves into what they considered spiritual ecstasy.

Then, as the sun set, the crowd began to disperse and the dervishes returned to the mosque. Many of the men in the audience entered the mosque as well, to join the evening prayers. Others returned to the tea ladies to have a hot drink.

Hanaan and Mia left immediately since Hanaan's driver was waiting for them in the car. Mia was grateful for the cool relief of the air-conditioning in the car, but she wanted to rid her mind of the chant and rhythm that still beat in her chest.

"What did you think?" Hanaan asked, as the car made a U-turn and headed back toward home.

"Well," Mia began. She did not want to offend Hanaan or the driver. "It was very . . . interesting." Mia hoped she never had to go there again.

"I think so too." Hanaan turned to face Mia. "What do you think about Mohammed?"

Mia froze. She knew that Mohammed was the Muslims' prophet and that they held him in high regard. She wanted to be truthful but, if she was, wouldn't she lose any further chance to share Jesus with Hanaan? Why couldn't her new friend start with a less explosive question? Mia prayed a silent prayer for wisdom and took a deep breath.

"I believe what he says about himself, Hanaan," Mia said. "Mohammed says that he is nothing special, that he is simply a warner, right?"

"Yes," Hanaan said, "*Alhamdullilah*, thanks be to Allah."

Mia glanced in the rearview mirror and noticed the driver was watching her. *Lord, please help me!*

"He says he does not know where he or his followers will be in the hereafter." Mia was thankful that Michael had insisted she read about Islam before moving to Sudan. "Well," she continued, "I also believe what Jesus says about himself. Jesus says, 'I am the Way, the Truth and the Life.' He is with God and whoever believes in Him will be with him forever. Hanaan, if I have to choose, I will choose the One who knows that He will be with God."

Silence filled the car. The driver's eyes darted back to the road. Hanaan continued to look at Mia intently. Mia stared at her lap, waiting for a verbal explosion. Or maybe a literal one; this was Sudan after all. But she felt empowered. That had surely been the Holy Spirit speaking. Was that what it felt like to be led by Him? Mia didn't care if there was a bomb. She knew the truth and God had given her the Arabic words to speak it. Still, she waited for a response.

Finally, Hanaan spoke.

"That's very interesting, Mia. I am glad you told me what you believe." Then, as if nothing significant had just happened, she leaned forward and spoke to the driver, "Pull over. I want you to get out and buy some oranges for me from that fruit stall before we go home."

They rode home in silence.

Thank you, Lord, for giving me the words to say. I'm sorry for doubting. Maybe I won't tell Michael I want to go home. Maybe if I just trust You ...

❖ CHAPTER 9 ❖

"*H*ello?" Mia answered the phone breathlessly.

"Hi Mia! It's Beth. Are you OK?"

"Oh, yes." Mia laughed. "I just ran to catch the phone. I was parking the car from being out . . . all morning. I've got stuff going on this evening too."

Why are you making sure Beth knows you are busy?

Beth didn't seem to notice.

"Oh, all right. Well, I wanted to see if you would go on a visit with me this Friday. I thought maybe Michael could watch the kids for you. It would be fun for you to have a chance to be around some Sudanese."

Mia felt instantly irritated. Why did Beth think Mia hadn't been around any Sudanese? She had, thank you very much. *Beth doesn't mean anything bad; she's just trying to help you. You were the one that told her you had trouble meeting Sudanese women.* Despite her flash of anger, she did really want to join her friend. Besides, she'd been with Sudanese Arabs for the past two Fridays, why stop now?

She swallowed her pride. "Sure, Beth, I'd love to go, thanks. I'll ask Michael if he can watch the kids."

He's not going to like this one bit.

Michael agreed to watch the kids, but Mia felt the tension between them rising when she asked him.

The following Friday, Beth and Mia rode a tickety city bus to Bahri and then walked toward the house of Beth's friend. The afternoon streets were a ghost town compared to the hustle and bustle of normal weekdays. The sun dropped heavy rays of heat on the shoulders and heads of the women as they strolled down the wide dirt road. Something about Fridays made people slow down a notch. It was a day to rest.

"I went to see Nafeesa yesterday," Beth said. "Raya and Muna are in intense pain from the circumcision." Beth's face tightened. Her eyes glistened with tears. "Muna won't eat or drink because she is afraid of going to the bathroom. While I was there, I helped Raya go to the bathroom. Mia, she was messed up. I don't think it will even heal into anything recognizable. Why do they do this to their children?"

"I am so sorry, Beth." What else could she say? "I've been doing some reading on the Internet about female circumcision since you told me about Nafeesa's girls. I learned the proper name is FGM: female genital mutilation. It appears that this tradition runs so deep that no one wants to be the first to take a stand against it. I read that, even though it seems like it is the men who want their wives and daughters to be circumcised, the reality is that it is the women who keep the tradition going."

"Yes," Beth said, wiping tears off her cheeks with the edge of the multi-colored scarf that covered her hair and hung gracefully off her shoulders. "The Kellar Hope office carries brochures about FGM. Those pamphlets say there are several levels of circumcision. They go from minor cutting to what is known as pharaonic circumcision, which is the removal of anything visible and then sewing the opening shut, except for a small hole, just big enough for urine and menstruation."

"I cannot imagine what husband and wife relations . . . or childbirth …" Mia could not finish her thought. This was not theoretical; this was reality for Nafeesa and her girls. Mia looked at the ground as they walked. Then she asked quietly, "What kind do Muna and Raya have?"

"Pharaonic," Beth said.

At the end of the long dusty road, Beth eyed a small shop that appeared to be open, even though it was Friday.

"Let's stop here," she said. "I want to buy some sugar to bring as a gift for my friends."

"Why sugar?" Mia asked.

"It is a great gift to bring because Sudanese serve sweet tea to all of their guests so they are always in need of it." She walked up the two stone steps to reach the counter of the little makeshift shop.

Mia stayed behind and studied her surroundings. The wide dusty street that they walked on was lined with brick walls. The bare walls crumbled, too old and dry to hold together. Three goats meandered along the street, nosing the ground for a piece of leaf or a blade of grass to nibble on. A group of young kids hovered over a toy car made of wood and bottle caps.

The sun glared down mercilessly, and Mia hurried up the steps to join Beth in the shade of the shop's awning. The shop was a dark, square room with very little inventory. Only the basics: bags of sugar, coffee beans, and fava beans lined the back wall and pyramids of canned milk powder and tomato paste filled a few shelves. On the front counter, a small cardboard box held a pile of chicken eggs.

"*Masa 'ilxayr,*" Beth called. Immediately, a portly gentleman in a white *jallabeeya* stuck his head through the back door of the shop. "*Jibni kilo sukar, lo semaht,*" said Beth in her near-perfect Arabic accent, "Please give me a kilo of sugar."

The jolly little man measured a kilo of the yellowish grains and poured them into a plastic bag.

"Where are you from?" he asked Beth.

"I am from Minnesota and my friend here is from Texas," she replied.

Mia knew that Beth avoided saying their country's name intentionally. Beth said it was because one could never be sure who was anti-American. Although Mia had only experienced the gracious hospitality of the Sudanese, she thought it would be a good idea for her to follow Beth's example.

"Ah!" the shopkeeper said, "Texas! Cowboy!" And with a grin he made his hands into pistols and shot them in the air, laughing heartily. Then he looked at Mia, but spoke to Beth, "Does she speak Arabic as well as you?"

"She speaks just a little," Beth replied.

Mia's ears burned. Beth had a lot of nerve judging Mia's Arabic right there in front of her. What gave her the right to grade her as "just a little"? What was that, like a D or an F?

If her face was bright red, the kind man didn't seem to notice. Instead, he eyed Beth's scarf and asked, "Are you Muslim?"

"Oh no," Beth said. "I follow *Isa alMasih*. Have you heard of him? You can read about him in the *Injil*, the New Testament."

Mia forgot her irritation with her friend and immediately began to pray. *Lord, please give Beth the words to say to this man.*

"Ah," the man said, "I have heard of it, but I have never read it."

Beth smiled. "I would like to give you one." She reached into her purse and pulled out a small black book. It was carefully wrapped in a white handkerchief, and she handed it to the man with both hands.

"*Shukran*," the man said, "Thank you."

"How much for the sugar?" Beth asked. The man told her the amount and she gave it to him.

As Beth and Mia turned to leave, the man said, "My name is Abbas and this is my home." He gestured to the living quarters behind his little store. "Please come back and meet my wife,

Widad, and our daughter, Yusra. You are welcome here anytime!"

Beth thanked him, and the two friends continued walking.

"That was great, Beth," Mia said, smiling. "That man has a New Testament now!"

"I know!" she said, excitement filling her voice. "I was going to give it to my friend today, but I think the Holy Spirit told me to give it to him instead."

"Yes, I know what that feels like! Just last week I think the Holy Spirit gave me words to say! I was talking with—"

"I think you should visit that man and his wife, Mia!" Beth interrupted, as if Mia weren't even talking. "I don't have time, what with all the visits I already make. Plus, you could meet his wife, what did he call her? Widad, that's it. You could practice your Arabic with her! Mia, this is perfect!"

Perfect. I already had a witnessing opportunity, Beth! I don't need you to set things up for me. And anyhow, my Arabic is just fine. I don't need your help! Ugh! Mia wanted to scream. She took a deep breath and forced a smile.

"That's a good idea, Beth."

Mia chided herself. Beth wasn't really being prideful; she did speak Arabic better than Mia. And she really did have too many visits to add another family to her schedule. Beth was right—this really was a great opportunity.

They walked in silence the rest of the way. While Beth was almost floating with excitement, Mia was floundering between emotions. Why was she like this? She had been calm and steady in Texas. Why was she so short-tempered in Sudan? If she just went ahead and told Michael she wanted to move back home, she wouldn't have to deal with how crazy Sudan made her feel. Maybe she could drop a few hints for him and see if he'd bite.

After all, Sudan wasn't worth giving up her sanity for.

When the women reached the house where Beth's friend lived, Mia was surprised that anyone lived there at all. The walls around the house were crumbling and, from where they stood at the gate, it looked like there was only one small room surrounded by the enclosure.

Beth knocked on the metal door that hung awkwardly from its hinges, pressed deep into the dried-mud wall. Mia warily eyed a donkey whose leg was tethered to an old tire. The poor creature looked like it might die at any moment. It looked back at her with sad eyes.

Beth said, "This is actually a better place than what this family had when they lived in the displacement camp. At least they have some privacy and their own toilet here."

Trying to avoid the donkey's gaze, Mia stared at the wall. The bricks were stacked and held together with mud, but they were not lined up evenly. The wall looked as if it would fall over. It was scorching hot. Sweat trickled down Mia's neck.

Finally, a teenage girl came to the door and peeked through the crack. When she saw Beth and Mia, her eyes brightened and she quickly opened the door.

"*Salaam aleykoom!*" Beth said as she shook Randa's hand and smiled. Randa ushered them through the tiny courtyard into a dark room. The mud and brick walls and the dirt floor cooled the room off a few noticeable degrees. On the bed lay a woman. Beth and Mia sat down on the bed adjacent to hers.

"Mom," Randa said. "It's Beth and a friend."

"Beth."

"*Salaam aleykum*, A'isha."

"*Aleykum wassalaam.*"

A'isha reached her hand out but barely turned her head. Beth grabbed her hand in a half handshake and kept holding it.

"I lost the babies."

"I know."

"I went to the hospital and had the babies last night. They died."

Beth began to speak to A'isha and Randa. Her Arabic flowed smoothly and both mother and daughter listened intently. Mia gathered that Beth was sharing a Bible story with them, although she couldn't exactly understand which one it was. How on earth did Beth get from her friend losing her babies to telling a Bible story so quickly?

I want to be able to do that. I need to get better at speaking Arabic.

After the story, Randa left the room and A'isha closed her eyes. Beth leaned toward Mia and spoke softly.

"A'isha and her family used to live out west in Darfur. The *jinjaweed* came to their village and they had to escape."

"What are *jinjaweed?*" Mia asked. She'd heard about the unrest in Darfur but was not familiar with that word.

"They are Arab fighters who ride on camels. They are known to be ruthless and are rumored to be armed with automatic weapons by the government itself. Families like A'isha's were in danger of being killed by their own Muslim brothers, simply because their blood is African, not Arab."

"That's why they moved to Khartoum?" Mia asked.

"Yes, it's safer for them here, although I think daily life is more difficult. They had to leave their farm and all their belongings behind so they really don't have anything here."

"Where is her husband?" Mia asked.

"He leaves early every morning to try to find work as a day laborer."

"Beth?" Randa called from outside where she was heating water for tea. Beth stood and went outside to join the teenager. Mia was left in the dark room with A'isha. She looked at the form lying on the bed across the room. Mia could not imagine the physical and emotional pain this poor woman was enduring.

Suddenly a thought came to her. This was her chance to show Jesus' love—the reason she came to Sudan. Beth had already told a Bible story, so obviously this woman didn't mind hearing about Jesus. If Mia couldn't muster confidence like Beth had, she shouldn't even be here.

Should I pray? Should I say something about God?

Before she could decide on what to do, Beth and Randa returned with glasses of tea. Mia thanked Randa and drank the tea, ignoring the fact that it was made with dirty water. She needed something to do with her mouth, since she wasn't using it to share the Good News of Jesus.

Beth, Mia, and Randa drank tea and visited while A'isha lay in bed, sometimes talking, sometimes closing her eyes and listening. Randa asked Mia where she was from and how many children she had.

"Your Arabic is very good!" Randa said.

"Oh, *shukran*, thank you!" Mia said. She sat a little taller on the bed and a new confidence seemed to flow into her veins. She participated more in the conversation than she had before, and she understood most of what Beth and Randa were saying.

Mia was engrossed in the experience and before she was ready, Beth said it was time to go. Beth asked A'isha if she could pray for her in the name of Jesus. A'isha nodded so Beth and Mia bowed their heads and Beth asked Jesus for healing for A'isha's body as well as her heart. When she was finished, A'isha reached her hand out and grabbed Beth's hand.

"*Shukran,*" she said.

During the prayer, Mia had rehearsed a sentence over and over in her head. She did not want to miss an opportunity to share Jesus with these precious Muslim women. As Beth and Mia said goodbye, Mia reached down and took A'isha's hand. She looked into the woman's eyes. She desperately wanted her to understand the importance of what she was going to say.

"A'isha, *Isa mukhabarat*. Jesus loves you. "

"*Shnoo?*" A'isha asked, "What?"

Mia smiled and spoke slowly and slightly louder, "*Isa mukhabarat.*" Then she sqeezed A'isha's hand gently and said, "*Wa ana bardo*. And I do too. "

Even a chance to share such a simple truth filled Mia's heart with joy. She was so happy that she had seized the opportunity. She did not notice the wrinkled eyebrows on Beth's face as they made their exit and walked away from A'isha's little mud home.

As they began walking down the street, Beth turned to Mia, her brow still furrowed.

"What did you mean, Mia?"

"About what?"

"What did you mean when you said that to A'isha?"

"Oh." Mia smiled. "I knew you'd told them a Bible story already, so I thought I'd also share a little bit. I told her Jesus loves her and so do I."

That was simple Arabic. Surely Beth had understood it. Mia looked up at her tall friend and saw her disturbed look disappear as she burst into laughter.

"What?" Mia asked.

"Did you mean to say '*Isa muhabba*'? As in, 'Jesus is love'?"

"Yes. Why is that funny?"

"Because you said '*mukhabarat*' instead of '*muhabba*' and that means 'secret police.' You told A'isha that Jesus is the secret police and so are you!"

❖ CHAPTER 10 ❖

*H*alimah sat on the cool tiles and gathered the notebooks that had been scattered on her bedroom floor for two weeks. "I can't believe we fooled my mother this whole time," she said.

Samia sat on the edge of the bed, folding her clothes and cramming them into her shoulder bag. "We didn't really lie, Halimah. We did make some wedding plans."

Halimah looked up at her friend and laughed. "Yea, about as many plans as our graduation committee has made!"

"Well, if I don't go home today, both of our mothers will get suspicious for sure. I'm feeling much better. I'm so glad I did this before Ramadan."

"A month of fasting would have been terrible in your condition. I tell you, you are a brave girl . . . what you did. It's going to be different for me, you know." Halimah shoved the stack of notebooks under her bed and leaned back against her friend's leg. "I am going to find a Sudanese man who works in Europe. I'm going to marry him and move away from this place."

Samia laughed. "Halimah! A Sudanese man is a Sudanese man, no matter where he lives."

"That's the thing," Halimah said, sitting up straight and turning around to look her friend in the eye. "I'll divorce him after we move to Europe. Then I'll be free to do as I please."

Samia playfully hit her with the folded blouse in her hand. "With whose money, my dear? We aren't like those Western women on TV, Halimah. We still need our men."

"Speak for yourself, Samia. I'm not getting my accounting degree for nothing. And that's another reason I've been learning English. I'm going to work and that will open more doors!"

"Yea, OK. Whatever. I gotta go, Halimah. If my mom calls before I get home, tell her I am on my way." Samia reached down and gave Halimah's shoulder a squeeze and then picked up her shoulder bag and left, almost bumping into Rania in the doorway.

"Halimah, I don't feel well," the younger girl said, ignoring Samia.

"Rania, that's rude. You should have said something to Samia. She's leaving, you know."

"Can I have my bed back then?" Rania sprawled on her bed before hearing the answer.

"I guess it doesn't matter either way, Rania. Why bother asking?" Halimah felt grumpy. Why couldn't she go to Europe and then get divorced? Or if her father couldn't find a man from Europe, why wouldn't a man in Sudan let her work? Ugh! Why did Samia resign so quickly to what society demanded of her? Even so, she'd gotten used to her best friend being around. Now she'd have to talk to Rania every night.

"Why don't you change the sheets first, Rania." There was no answer. Halimah glanced over Rania's shoulder and saw that her little sister's eyes were closed and she was breathing deeply. Good grief, she really must have been tired. Halimah took the sheets off her own bed and flipped off the light switch as she left the room. Rania would just have to wash her own sheets later.

Halimah had been neglecting her religion lately. Samia was not faithful at her prayers, and her laziness had rubbed off on Halimah. Now that Ramadan was just a few days away, she determined to be better. Maybe not praying five times a day, but any little bit helped, right?

Today was a good day to begin her new habit. Samia was gone and Rania was napping. Halimah grabbed her prayer mat that hung on her bedrail and took it to the water faucet in the front courtyard. Placing her mat to the side, she leaned over and twisted the faucet. Hot water sizzled out of the nozzle for a few seconds and then cooled off. Halimah stuck her hands under the faucet and let the coolness run over her palms.

"*Bismillah,*" she muttered under her breath. "In the name of Allah."

She continued to let the water run over her hands and wrists and in between her fingers. *It's a good thing Ramadan is upon us,* Halimah thought. *Maybe I'll find some peace.*

She cupped her right hand and scooped water into her mouth to rinse and spit.

I feel like there's a hole in my heart. Maybe fasting each day of Ramadan will help me refocus.

She held her cupped hand up to her nose and sniffed in some of the water. Doing so always made her choke but—this time especially—she wanted to be clean before she prayed. She had to get some peace in her heart. She sniffed water into her nose and blew it out three times.

Abdu is so vigilant with his prayers. Maybe I should start joining him at the mosque.

Halimah cupped both hands this time and splashed her face. Remembering her lessons in *wudhu*—washing before prayer—as a child, she was careful to wash from ear to ear and from her forehead to her chin.

Halimah thought about Ramadan. For one month every year, Muslims fasted during the daylight hours to earn favor with Allah. She had always looked forward to Ramadan. Her favorite part was '*Iftaar*, the breaking of the fast at sundown. '*Iftaar* was a special time for Halimah's family. Each evening she would help Mama prepare a meal. When the *muezzin* announced over the loud speaker—at every mosque across the city—that the day's fast was over, Halimah's family would eat together. Sometimes Father invited friends or family to join them. Sometimes they would pile into Father's car and go to a relative's house. But always, they ate together.

Halimah wanted to care more about the religious meaning of Ramadan. She leaned over the faucet and let the water run up each arm. With her hands she guided the water up to her elbows. She ran her wet hands over her head, front to back, and all around her ears.

Wudhu is only symbolic. I'm not really getting my head or ears clean by doing this. She was surprised by her own thoughts. Were her doubts negating her actions? Did she need to begin *wudhu* all over again? *I wish there was a way to get this water on the inside of me.* Her unruly thoughts were taking over again. *It's the inside I'm worried about, not the outside.*

Halimah stuck her feet, one at a time, under the water and washed up to her ankles. Then she unfolded her prayer mat and laid it on the veranda, facing a purple bougainvillea on the east side of the yard. Softly, she recited the obligatory confession of belief as she positioned herself at one end of her mat. She began her prayers by greeting the angels on her right and left shoulders. They kept track of her good and bad deeds. She wondered if they were keeping tabs on her actions only, or if they had heard her thoughts as well.

The familiarity of tradition comforted her heart. She rose and knelt on the mat just the way she'd done all her life. Just the way her mother before her had done, and her *haboba* before that. There was something about tradition. Maybe it didn't fill the void in her heart, but it gave her something to hold onto something familiar during a time when her thoughts were charting strange territories.

At mid-day Rania was asleep, and Halimah wondered if she really might be sick or if she was just trying to get attention now that Samia was gone. Talk at lunch circled around Ramadan. Halimah ate quietly and listened to her parents make plans for who might eat *'Iftaar* with them. Ali, small and wiry little boy that he was, told a story of how he won a fight against Basim, a much bigger neighborhood boy. Father scolded him—but only a little. Halimah could see that the man's eyes sparkled with pride over this son who could make a name for himself among his peers.

Halimah listened and tried to appear interested. Inside, she felt a twinge of worry, an unsettled stirring in the pit of her stomach. Why wasn't she excited about Ramadan like she had been in years past? Sure, she was hoping to earn some merit by her prayers and her fasting this month, but where was the joy?

She felt all mixed up. Was it because she had begun to read the *Injil* more? Was that the cause for her lackluster emotions? Halimah hardly dared to admit it to herself, but sometimes she read the book for hours. At night, after Rania and Samia were asleep, she pulled the sheets over her head and turned on a flashlight to read. Even though she originally read the book to help her with English, it had been several weeks since she read that side of the page. Instead, she focused on the Arabic. She found that her desire to learn the message of the *Injil* had become stronger than her desire to practice English.

"Halimah!" Mama interrupted her thoughts, making her jump.

"Yes?" She smiled, trying to appear calm.

Mama tilted her head and gave her an inquisitive look. Then she shook her head, as if to say, *Young people! Who can understand them?* "Why don't you take some food to Rania? It seems as if she plans to spend the day in her room."

"Yes, Mama," Halimah replied, thankful for an excuse to leave the colorless lunch conversation. She picked up an empty plate and filled it with fried meat, tomatoes, and two chick pea fritters. Adding a piece of bread, she hastily left the room.

Rania never ate the food.

That evening Mama came to the bedroom again to check on her youngest daughter. She leaned her big body over the small girl and felt her forehead with her palm.

"She's feverish, Halimah," said the woman. She looked over to where her eldest daughter sat on her bed, feigning interest in an accounting textbook. "You'll need to stay awake and keep an eye on her," she said. She crossed the room, and kissed Halimah on the top of her head. Then she picked up the plate on the end of Rania's bed—still full of food from lunch—and left the room.

Halimah decided to keep herself awake by reading. She laid aside her textbook and tiptoed to the wardrobe to retrieve the *Injil.* Her favorite part of the whole book was the section called "Romans." How strange to claim that righteousness came from God through faith in Jesus Christ and that it was available for anyone who believed. Halimah had been taught, from the time she was just a child, that her good works were what would give her hope for heaven. And she tried to do enough good works to outweigh her sins, but who could really know for sure? Abdu was definitely better at following the Five Pillars of Islam, but Halimah knew that Abdu drank alcohol. Wasn't that bad enough to negate all his prayers?

The *Injil* said in Romans 3:22–24, "There is no difference, for all have sinned and fall short of the glory of God, and are justified freely by his grace through the redemption that came by Christ Jesus." This was strange. What was meant by grace? And what did it mean to be *justified freely*?

Then there were the stories about *Isa*. Halimah knew He was a prophet. But the *Injil* said that He was God's Son and that He had great power. He loved people and treated them kindly. The stories were beautiful. Jesus healed and taught people—even women.

Halimah spent most of the night reading. She knew she should stop. She knew, if anything, she should be reading the Qur'an. It was dangerous to be reading this book.

❖ CHAPTER II ❖

"Rania definitely has malaria," Mama announced when she came to check on the girls the next morning.

Halimah was still in bed, exhausted from staying awake most of the night. As her mother leaned over her little sister's bed, Halimah realized that her *Injil* lay in plain sight beside her on the bed. Her heart skipped a beat. She must have fallen asleep while reading. She grabbed it and stuffed it under her pillow. Mama was still fussing over Rania.

"This will never do; she's burning hot. I will call Father home from work, and we'll take her to the hospital to get tested. Abdu is at work and Ali is at school. Halimah, you stay home. I'll need you to help take care of Rania when we get back."

"Yes, Mama," she replied, grateful not to be forced to get up and get dressed. She felt like she'd been run over by a donkey cart.

While Mama made the phone call, Halimah arose and returned the *Injil* to its spot in the wardrobe. She glanced at Rania. Her face was as pale as a *khawadja's*, one of those white people they watched on TV shows. She looked limp and her clothes were drenched in sweat.

When Mama returned, they changed the listless girl into a fresh housedress. The fever had broken and she was cold and clammy. Her thin body shivered. Halimah felt a twinge of regret for being so grumpy around her sister. She was obviously very ill. Halimah touched her arm; it was limp and lifeless.

"What if she dies?"

"Halimah! Don't say such a thing. What is wrong with you, child?"

Oh, no! She hadn't meant to say that out loud. Her thoughts were running away from her again, and now they were escaping her mouth!

"I'm sorry, Mama. I'm just scared."

"It's malaria," her mother said matter of factly. The large woman heaved the shivering girl into her arms like she was a little child. She walked determinedly from the room and out of the house.

Mothers, they have the strength of an ox when it comes to taking care of their children. Halimah wondered if she would be like that one day. She always wanted to be a mother. Except for lately, when she'd decided to move to Europe and then get divorced. But that would never happen. She would eventually have to give up that dream and marry the man her father chose for her. She'd have babies and raise children. She would do well to give up the *Injil* along with her dreams. It would be better to give it all up now, before Ramadan, so that she could concentrate on fasting and praying.

When Halimah was a child, her grandmother taught her to braid hair. *Haboba* would sit on a metal bed in the *hosh*, the courtyard, while the girl getting the braids—usually a granddaughter—sat on a short stool in front of her. Halimah would watch the old woman, sitting so close to her that their hips touched. When *Haboba's* elbows would knock Halimah in the head, the old woman would chuckle.

"Child, move over before I knock you out!"

Halimah would scoot over, but just a little. She didn't want to miss anything. *Haboba* held a comb in her mouth while she divided the girl's hair into sections. Then she divided those sections into even smaller sections, carefully parting with the comb that she took from between her teeth. Her fingers would glide quickly across the scalp. Halimah marveled at how effortlessly she created beautiful lines, straight and tight, across the head of her cousin. If she had a colored band, *Haboba* would tie the ends, but there really was no need, as the kinky hair tangled quickly into a tight hold on the finished braids. Halimah looked at the rows of braids, admiring her grandmother's skill.

"See how the rows are neat and straight, Halimah," she would say. "You have to braid fast, or you could sit here all day long just for one person's braids."

One day, *Haboba* grabbed Halimah's hands, one soft little hand in each of her tough, wrinkled ones. "Lines are from Allah, *habeebtee*. You can never forget Allah; His mark is on you." Then she turned Halimah's little hands so that her palms faced up, "Read them, *habeebtee*. The ninety-nine names of Allah, on your hands. Look at your left hand."

Halimah saw the upside-down *V* and the *I*, the script used for numbers eight and one.

"Eight and one make nine. Now look at your right hand."

Halimah saw the *I* and the upside-down *V*.

"One and eight make nine."

Haboba traced the wrinkle lines on the young girl's palms with her rough index finger.

"Ninety-nine, Halimah."

Halimah knew that her grandmother could not read. *Haboba* did not even know her numbers. But the old woman had learned this from her father, and he from his father, and on and on.

"You were born a Muslim and your family is known as a good Muslim family. You will always be Muslim, Halimah."

Allah's ninety-nine names were written on her hands. Halimah thought that they must be on every Muslim's hands. Were they on *Haboba's* hands? She couldn't tell because *Haboba's* palms were very wrinkly.

"*Haboba,* Allah must have a thousand names on your hands."

Haboba laughed. "You are a smart girl. You should memorize the Qur'an. You would be very good at that. I will speak to your mother about it."

Halimah didn't want to memorize the Qur'an. That sounded like a lot of work. But if it made *Haboba* happy, she would do it.

"Rania does not have malaria," Mama said. Her voice quivered with worry as Halimah's father laid the young girl gently on her bed. Halimah had changed Rania's bed sheets to fresh ones while she was gone, and she sat down on the edge of the bed beside her. The fever had returned; she could feel the heat, even without touching Rania's body.

"What are we going to do?" Halimah asked.

"There is nothing we can do," her father replied. "The doctor doesn't know what she has."

She had never seen Father look helpless until that moment. His shoulders drooped, his dress shirt was damp with sweat, his brow wrinkled. Mama switched into busy mode shooing her husband out of the room.

"You go change into a clean shirt and go back to work. Halimah and I will take care of Rania. Halimah!" Mama yelled, even though Halimah was standing behind her. Suddenly noticing her, Mama said, "Get a bowl of cool water and a cloth. We'll try to stop her fever that way."

Halimah and Father obeyed without protest.

Halimah stayed awake most of the night. Every hour she would refill a bowl with cool water and dip a cloth in it to press on Rania's forehead. Despite her earlier thoughts about giving up the

Injil, she continued to read it. She had to do something to stay awake. In her bed she read under her covers.

Suddenly, her flashlight seemed to flicker on the page, making some of the words glow. Halimah stared at the book. She shook her flashlight, then turned it off. She looked back at the book and the words were still glowing. She read Ephesians 2:8: "For it is by grace you have been saved, through faith—and this not from yourselves, it is the gift of God—not by works, so that no one can boast."

Saved by grace? Saved through faith? What about all the work I do to be good? What about fasting and praying and my family's good name? As Muslims, we don't know for sure whether we will go to heaven or not. We do the best we can and hope Allah will be merciful. Can I really be assured that I will go to heaven by believing in Jesus, in Isa? No one in my family believes that. It would be shameful for me to believe it. And yet, somehow, I think I do believe it.

Rania groaned from across the room. Halimah slipped the *Injil* under her pillow and went to tend to her little sister. She dipped the cloth in the bowl, squeezed it, and placed it on her sister's forehead. Rania whimpered. Halimah had an idea. She didn't know if it was a good idea or not, but it was worth a try.

She took the book from under her pillow and flipped to the section that she knew had stories about *Isa.* She read a story to Rania. It was a story about *Isa* healing a little girl who was dead.

"Don't be afraid," Jesus had said, "just believe." When she finished the story, she looked at Rania. The girl had stopped whimpering and was asleep.

Could Jesus heal Rania? Halimah placed her hand on her sister's feverish forehead and in a soft but audible voice said, "Jesus, if You will heal Rania, then I will believe that You are God."

Halimah closed the *Injil* and put it back in the wardrobe. She went to her own bed and crawled under the covers. She squeezed her eyes shut. She thought she should probably pray more, but exhaustion from two mostly sleepless nights overtook her body and she fell asleep.

❖ CHAPTER 12 ❖

The sun trickled in the window of Halimah's and Rania's room, casting dancing patterns onto the tile floor. Halimah blinked a few times, trying to force away the blur of sleep. She heard a sound from across the room. She rolled over and looked toward Rania's bed. There was her little sister, sitting up, smiling weakly.

"Can I have some water, *'ukhti*, my sister? And maybe I could eat some bread."

Time froze. Halimah's head was spinning. She threw the covers off and sat up quickly.

It is true! Jesus has power! He truly is the Son of God.

Within minutes, the whole family was in the bedroom celebrating. Even Abdu came in to kiss Rania and, for once, Ali was not a brat. He helped by bringing some food for his recovering sister.

"What happened during the night, Halimah? How did Rania suddenly get well?" Mama asked. Halimah saw the eyes of her whole family turn toward her. Oh dear, she wasn't ready for this.

"I was sleeping," she stammered, "well, I was watching her and I was . . . praying."

At this, she saw Abdu stand up straight and look very proud. He was surely congratulating himself for training his sister to pray.

Not satisfied with her answer, Father turned to Rania. "Rania, do you know what happened?"

Did she? Had she heard Halimah reading the *Injil* to her? Halimah had known at the time that it was dangerous, but she seemed to be defying danger lately. She held her breath and watched her sister.

"I don't know, Father," she said.

"Well, *alhamdullilah* you are well. We are so thankful, *habeebtee*." He leaned down and kissed her head.

The family left the bedroom and the girls were alone again. After her breakfast, Rania was tired and needed to sleep again.

"I am going to sleep too, Rania. You just tell me if you need something. And Rania?"

"Yes, *'ukhti?*"

"I'm really glad you are well." Halimah laid with her back to Rania and prayed. *Jesus, you healed my sister. I believe the Injil, and I believe that it is by faith in You, not by my good works, that I can be forgiven of my sins.* That was it. That was all she knew to say. She hoped it was all right to pray while curled up in bed. It seemed very disrespectful and would never be allowed in Islam. She wasn't even facing east. But it was the only way she could think of to pray to Jesus without getting in trouble with her family. And somehow, even without performing *wudhu*, she knew that her heart was cleaner than it had ever been.

Halimah got off the bus a few blocks from the church. She chose a church far away from her house. She didn't want any acquaintances to see what she was doing. She tried to appear confident as she walked toward the building which had crosses painted on its outside walls. *Perhaps those were like the Cross that Jesus died on.*

Halimah swallowed hard and kept walking toward the building. If it was proven that she had become a Christian, Halimah could be killed. She looked around her anxiously, but she was a stranger in this part of town and no one was paying any attention to her. For once, Halimah was thankful that her skin was a shade darker than most Arabs. She pulled a pair of sunglasses out of her purse and put them on, hoping that she would pass for a Southerner. Many Southern Sudanese were Christians, so the government had allowed a handful of churches to be built in Khartoum. As long as Halimah looked like a Southern Sudanese, she could enter one of their churches without getting into trouble.

Since when have I ever wished to be a Southerner? I was raised to hate them!

Slipping through the doors of the church building, Halimah quickly sat on the back row. It was Sunday and that was the day she had seen churches open. If she believed in Jesus, she would have to come to a church like this on Sundays. Where else would she learn more about her new belief?

Halimah listened with delight to the beautiful songs. She could read the words from the book that sat on the bench beside her. The blessing pronounced by the man in the front was strange, like nothing she had ever heard.

"The Lord bless you and keep you; the Lord make His face shine upon you and be gracious to you; the Lord turn His face toward you and give you peace."

The sermon seemed strange too, and Halimah couldn't look for the Scriptures that were mentioned because she had been too afraid to bring her copy of the *Injil*. But the preacher seemed to encourage people to look up the Scriptures and read for themselves, even after the service. The *sheikh* at Halimah's neighborhood mosque never encouraged people to look up truths for themselves. Abdu always just listened and believed anything he said without question.

"Don't believe me," this preacher said. "Look for yourself!"

Halimah had never been allowed to just read for herself and decide what she believed. Her mind wandered to *Haboba*.

"The ninety-nine names of Allah are on your hands, Halimah. You are a Muslim—you are always a Muslim."

Maybe the wrinkles that formed the number ninety-nine are on everyone's hands. Maybe they are just wrinkles, like the lines on the soles of my feet.

When the service was over, Halimah reached into her purse to retrieve her sunglasses and slip out. But a small woman slipped into Halimah's row and sat on the long wooden bench beside her. It was the teacher from the university, the one who had given Halimah the *Injil*.

"What are you doing here?" Halimah squeaked, happy to see a familiar face.

"The question is, what are *you* doing here?" the teacher asked.

"I read the book you gave me," Halimah replied. She felt her fears melting. "And I believe it. You are the first person I have told."

"Halimah, I am so happy for you. Jesus is the truth. I am so glad you believe in Him."

"Me too," Halimah said. Her heart was dancing. Not only did she feel free and forgiven, she had a new friend here at church.

"Halimah," the teacher said, placing a hand on her arm, "you can't come here. It's not safe for you."

Halimah frowned. "I have to."

"No, you don't have to go to a church building to worship Jesus. There are house groups that are safer for people like you."

"People like me?" Halimah knew that she meant Sudanese Arabs. Everyone knew it was illegal for a Muslim to convert. Everyone knew that Sudanese Arabs were Muslim.

I guess my disguise didn't work as well as I thought.

The teacher smiled at her and patted her arm. "It's OK, my sister, it's better for you this way." She took a piece of paper out of her purse and scribbled something on it. She folded it and handed it to Halimah.

"This is the name and number of a pastor. He leads a house meeting with other people who believe. You can go to this meeting and learn about Jesus, and it would be much safer for you."

Halimah hugged her new friend goodbye, knowing that she would probably never see her again. She slipped the sunglasses on and left the church. As she walked away from the building, she felt the eyes of a million Arabs looking at her, condemning her. She could almost hear her father's phone ringing with reports of people who saw his daughter enter a church building. She felt unnerved and picked up her pace. The teacher was right. This had not been a smart idea.

❖ CHAPTER 13 ❖

*H*alimah didn't want to fast when Ramadan arrived. She read about fasting in the *Injil*. Even Jesus fasted. But Halimah did not want to fast with the Muslims. She was not a follower of Mohammed anymore.

The first week of Ramadan was easy. Abdu caught her eating in the kitchen after sunrise and she smiled at him. "I'm on my period," she said. For once, she was telling the truth. Women could not fast or pray during that time. Halimah was free to eat for the whole first week. It was the following three weeks that she wasn't so sure about. She'd have to be more careful then.

The university was closed for the month of Ramadan. Halimah had no reason to be out of the house, as far as her father was concerned. She spent most of her days helping Mama cook. They fried fish from the Nile, made *kifta*, *sambosas*, cut fresh vegetables for salads and, of course, often made traditional *aseeda*.

"I'll go buy the *kisra*," Halimah would say, offering to buy the bread that would be served with the meal.

"No." Mama would shake her head. "Let Ali do it."

Did she know that Halimah had gone to the church? Were Mama and Father going to keep her home even after Ramadan was over?

Each evening, the house was full of guests. After the meal, Halimah boiled water in the kettle, plopping two cinnamon sticks inside and some cardamom pods too. When the water bubbled, she prepared her Mama's good silver tray with the nice cups and saucers that her father liked to use for guests. She served tea and cookies to her father's guests.

Father would look proudly at her when she entered the room. She knew that he was looking for a husband for her. He had made friends with a wealthy businessman who had a son about the marrying age, but he was also waiting to hear back from Halimah's cousin Abdul Rahman. Being the eldest cousin of marrying age, he had first choice. If he refused, then her father would be free to discuss marriage with a non-relative. Halimah hoped Abdul Rahman would say no.

When Sunday arrived, Halimah asked Mama if she could go to meet with the graduation committee. It was a lie. She said it quickly, before she even thought. Lying was a hard habit to stop. Her mother said yes. Halimah was relieved. Surely this meant that she had not heard about Halimah's visit to a church.

"I'll be back in time to help you cook for '*iftaar*,'" Halimah promised as she headed out the door.

A hot breeze carrying grains of sand blew against her as she shut the gate and began to walk down the street. She walked toward the bus stop to avoid suspicion. As she walked, she absently stuck her hand in the pocket of her *abaya* and felt the piece of paper with the pastor's name on it. Mansur. Halimah had memorized both the name and the phone number in case she had to get rid of it quickly. But no one had found it, and today she would call the number.

Halimah walked to the end of the street, turned left, and kept walking. She didn't know where she was going. She spotted the open area surrounding the neighborhood mosque. Halimah had played there many times as a little girl. The grounds were wide and spacious back then with lots of room to run. Now it seemed small and crowded. Had it changed, or had she changed?

Stick-and-burlap dwellings dotted the area. A few Beja families occupied them. They had moved to Khartoum from Port

Sudan and were too poor to have their own house. The *sheikh* at the mosque let them squat on the property. Only the husbands left to go to the market or to socialize. The young mothers only spoke Bedawi, stayed in their tents, and raised their children. The kids tended goats that grazed for bits of greenery on the bone-dry shrubs and acacia trees scattered around the mosque compound.

Halimah walked past the tents and stood among the goats. She took her cell phone from her purse and dialed the number from memory.

Halimah hadn't written anything down for fear that Father or Abdu would find it. She rehearsed the directions in her head:

"Thursday at eleven in the morning. The main road into Haj Yusif, first right after the shop with the blue walls. Fifth gate on the left after the empty lot."

Halimah counted the gates as she walked. She noticed a mixture of Nuba Mountain people and Arabs on the street. All of them looked Muslim. The men wore white *jallabeeyas,* and the women and girls were covered in colorful *tobes.* The Nuba Mountain people were dark-skinned, just like Southerners. The Arabs were lighter skinned with sharper features. No one took notice of Halimah as she approached the fifth gate and knocked lightly.

A young girl, perhaps seven or eight years old, answered the door and looked up at Halimah with wide eyes. She didn't move to let Halimah in until they both turned at the voice of Mansur.

"It's all right, Amina, you can let her in. Halimah! I am so glad you could come!"

Halimah looked over the girl's head at the approaching man. She recognized Mansur's deep voice from the phone call. She had expected him to be Southern Sudanese, so his light skin and his white *jalabeeya* surprised her. Only Muslims wore the white robes.

Was Mansur Sudanese Arab? Could it be that she was not the only Sudanese Arab that believed in Jesus? Halimah looked down at Amina and smiled. Amina giggled and opened the gate to let her in, then glanced out at the street quickly before shutting the gate.

Mansur ushered Halimah across the dirt courtyard and into a small room full of plastic chairs. The room was dark, with only light from the open door and the windows. Halimah squinted and looked around.

Four men and two women sat in the plastic chairs in a semi-circle, facing Halimah and Mansur who stood in the doorway. At first glance, Halimah calculated that one or two of them might be Arab and the rest Nuba mountain people. Halimah guessed from Mansur's accent, now confirmed by his features and clothes, that he was Arab.

At the church that Halimah had visited, the men wore slacks and dress shirts while the women wore dresses and occasionally long pants. Halimah had noticed that some of the teen girls hadn't even covered their hair. Looking around the group at this house, Halimah felt comfortable even though the people were strangers. The men were dressed just like Halimah's father, and the women were wearing *tobes*.

"I'd like you to meet Halimah. She is a new sister of ours," Mansur said in his rich and confident voice.

"*Salaam aleykum,*" Halimah said with all the courage she could muster. She imagined they might be scared of her. She was scared too. Since leaving Islam was illegal in Sudan, letting strangers know she had converted from Islam was risky. Mansur had assured her that this group consisted of people who used to be Muslim but now followed Jesus. They certainly dressed like Muslims.

To Halimah's surprise, every person in the room smiled warmly. They greeted her with handshakes, and one of the women offered Halimah the empty chair next to her. Halimah sat down, thankful to be out of the spotlight. Little Amina, who had disappeared after opening the gate for Halimah, appeared again with a tray of dry dates. Behind her was another woman, perhaps the woman of the house. She was carrying a tray of tea glasses.

While the woman and Amina distributed glasses of steaming hot tea and offered dates, the members of the group introduced themselves to Halimah. How strange, she thought, that men and women could sit together in the same room to worship Jesus. At the mosque, the women always sat behind a curtain so that they could hear the *sheikh* preach but could not be seen by the men. Even at the church she visited the week before, the men sat on one side of the room and the women sat on the other.

The woman of the house and Amina sat down after inviting everyone to drink the tea. Mansur quietly shut the door to the room and flipped the switch to a single light bulb that dangled from the ceiling.

The room grew stifling, but Halimah preferred the stuffiness to the possibility of Mansur's deep voice being heard by people on the street. He began the meeting with a prayer, thanking God for the freedom to meet together and for Halimah's new life.

Are we really free? I had to sneak away to come here today, and we are hiding in a hot, dark room. Why won't our country let us worship in the open? Halimah marveled at Mansur's thankful prayer.

The group sang a song together. The melody was beautiful. Halimah determined to memorize the words. Perhaps the nice woman sitting beside her would write the lyrics for her to look at. As they sang, Amina disappeared again and reappeared with a stack of books that looked like Halimah's *Injil*.

The woman sitting next to Halimah leaned over and spoke softly. "Ghada, Amina's mother, keeps Bibles here at her house so that we can use them for worship without having to keep them in our home or carry them back and forth."

"Won't she get in trouble for keeping so many in her house?" Halimah asked.

"Yes, she might."

Mansur began speaking, and the women turned their attention to him.

"How is everyone doing this week? Did you get a chance to share Jesus with anyone?"

Without hesitation, people began to speak about their experiences over the past week. One man shared that a relative had died and this gave him an opportunity to share about Jesus' power over death. Little Amina asked the group to pray for her because her friends made fun of her at school because she wouldn't cheat on a test. Ghada said she was so thankful to have made enough money this week to pay for her electric bill.

Halimah glanced at the bare bulb hanging above them. Her family had never been poor. In fact, Halimah had always had whatever she wanted. Father just handed her money whenever she asked. Had she ever been thankful for anything as simple as the money to light a room?

After a few more minutes of sharing, Mansur prayed for the whole group. Then he encouraged everyone to take a Bible and open it to Colossians 3. Halimah let her new friend beside her help find the passage. The whole group read the passage together, each person reading a verse until the whole chapter was read. Could men and women really read the Word of God and learn together like this?

The group began to discuss the passage. To her relief, no one pressured Halimah to say anything. As she listened, though, she imagined herself participating. Yes, perhaps the next time she joined them she would say something. She could feel the love and acceptance in this group, and it was a very different feeling from what she felt when she prayed at the mosque, where rules and regulations dictated every activity.

"Now," Mansur said, "what will you do differently this week? How has this passage from Colossians changed you?"

Amina was the first to speak. "This week I will be thankful that I don't have to cheat. Instead of crying when the kids laugh at me, I will pray for them and forgive them."

How was it that a young child was taken so seriously in a worship meeting? Amina was probably still in elementary school. Halimah thought of Rania who would also like to be taken seriously. Halimah remembered the words they had just read from Colossians, "clothe yourselves with compassion, kindness, humility, gentleness and patience."

"I would like to be kinder to my younger sister." Halimah was surprised by her own voice.

"Who would like to pray for Amina and Halimah?" Mansur asked.

The woman beside Halimah raised her hand and immediately bowed her head. "We are called to live in peace with everyone," she began. "Jesus, we ask You to give Amina and Halimah the courage this week to do this very thing with their friends and family. We ask that because of their courage, others will see Your love in them. We know that's how the Gospel will spread in this country. Thank you, Jesus."

Two hours passed quickly. She wasn't ready to go home; she wanted to stay with this group longer.

"Come back next week, Halimah," Mansur said.

"I will, thank you."

The group left Ghada's house in ones and twos.

"We don't want to draw attention," Ghada explained to Halimah. "My family is Muslim, and they don't know that we are meeting here."

"Won't someone find out? Or see your Bibles?" Halimah asked.

"My husband has recently taken a second wife," Ghada said. "He has moved to Wad Medani to live with her. He doesn't come to see us very often." Ghada looked down at her young daughter. She smiled and placed her hand on Amina's shoulder. "But that frees us to worship Jesus without hindrance."

"Well," Halimah said, "thank you for letting me worship with you."

"You are welcome anytime, Halimah."

"I'll pray for you this week, that you will be kind to your little sister," Amina said.

"Thank you, Amina!"

Halimah slipped through the gate and back out onto the street. Her steps were light, and she couldn't wipe the grin off of her face. She was in love: in love with Jesus and in love with His children.

Samia was preoccupied with wedding plans so it was easy for Halimah to avoid the subject of her new belief. The hard part was not joining her friend in deceiving their fathers anymore. During past Ramadans, the friends would tell their fathers that they were going to hear Sheikh Maymoun preach at his mosque. Halimah's father was always very eager to let her go.

"Sheikh Maymoun is one of my favorite preachers," he would say.

Sheikh Maymoun also happened to be long-winded. Samia and Halimah would wait for 'Isra and Zainab outside the mosque and agree on a time to meet back there. Then they would go their separate ways. 'Isra and Zainab left to meet up with boys. Samia and Halimah went wandering through the market and enjoyed feeling free. After about an hour and a half, the four girls would regroup at the mosque and walk home together.

But things were different now. Halimah didn't meet her friends to go to the mosque. She told them she was using the month of Ramadan to study for finals. When she could get away from the house, she attended whatever prayer group or home church Mansur was leading.

Mansur lent her some books about Jesus. Halimah hid them with her copy of the *Injil* and devoured them when Rania fell asleep at night. She also learned songs at the meetings. They had beautiful lyrics that praised God in such a wonderful way:

> *"Heaven for eternity!*
> *Jesus paid the debt for me!*
> *Daily walking in His love,*
> *Together we shall overcome.*
> *There is no punishment or hell*
> *for me, and I will live to tell:*
> *His blood will cleanse all who believe."*

Halimah sang quietly as she made the beds in Abdu's bedroom. It still amazed her that it was not by her works that she would earn the right to enter heaven. No one deserved heaven; how could she ever hope to earn it? But Jesus had paid her debt and it was by His merciful sacrifice that she could go to heaven. What a gift!

She sang the words of the song again.

"That's a beautiful song, Halimah! Will you teach it to me?"

Halimah's stomach jumped to her throat. She whirled around to see Rania standing in the doorway.

"Oh, Rania! You scared me! Come, help me make Abdu's bed. He's such a slob, you know." Halimah's father would most certainly beat the two of them if Rania were caught singing a song about Jesus. "Let me teach you one from *Haboba*, it's a silly song and you'll like it." She sang the bits she remembered and made up a few lines for the parts she forgot.

"It's OK," Rania said, "but not like the other song you were singing."

Rania turned and left the bedroom. Halimah stayed to gather the dirty clothes tossed on the floor. She was bending down to pick up the last pair of trousers when she felt a presence enter the room. She stood, but her back was to the door. Before she could turn around, she felt a shadow across her shoulder. Abdu leaned down and whispered in her ear.

"I heard the words you were singing. If I hear you sing them again, I will tell Father. He will beat you."

❖ CHAPTER 14 ❖

*M*ia's alarm clock went off at six a.m. She rolled out of bed and stumbled across the room and into the kitchen to flip on the coffee maker. While waiting for the coffee to brew, she sat at the kitchen table and opened her Bible to the Gospel of Luke.

She read Luke 21:12–19, "But before all this, they will lay hands on you and persecute you. They will deliver you to synagogues and prisons, and you will be brought before kings and governors, and all on account of my name. This will result in your being witnesses to them. But make up your mind not to worry beforehand how you will defend yourselves. For I will give you words and wisdom that none of your adversaries will be able to resist or contradict. You will be betrayed even by parents, brothers, relatives and friends, and they will put some of you to death. All men will hate you because of me."

Mia scooped two generous spoonfuls of powder creamer into a coffee mug and filled the rest with dark, hot coffee. She sat back down and sipped the rich beverage as she thought about the passage. *Was Jesus talking about the things that His disciples would go through, or did His warning reach through the ages to touch my generation?*

Persecution was not a foreign concept in Sudan. Conversion from Islam to Christianity was illegal. Mia remembered reading that the punishment for those who converted to Christianity was most often administered by the family. They could beat, disown, or even kill a family member who left Islam. Few cases ever went to court. Was this what Jesus was talking about?

Oh, Lord, give strength to those who want to believe in You but are afraid of their families. I know You have many people in this city who have placed their faith in Jesus as the Way, the Truth, and the Life. But they face immense difficulty—much more than I can imagine. Please give them a place of honor in Your kingdom. Please, Lord, help them remain strong and faithful to You, even as You remain faithful to them!

Then Mia's thoughts turned to those who were not Christians. Millions of Sudanese were Muslim.

I pray for those people to see the truth. Mia's words did not match the feeling in her heart. She felt like someone was shooting little pellets of doubt into her soul.

Can the power of God reach down through the thick darkness? Do my prayers break through the cloud? God, I know that with You all things are possible, but my heart doesn't feel it and my eyes don't see it. My ears don't hear it.

Mia sighed and looked at the coffee dregs in the bottom of her cup. Why did her prayer times often end in discouragement?

"Good morning, Dear!" Michael said as he walked into the kitchen. "What's with the serious face?"

"Oh," Mia forced a smile. "Just thinking through some stuff."

"So early in the morning?" Michael chuckled as he poured a mug of coffee. His back was to her. She noticed absently that the muscles in his arm flexed as he lifted the carafe, tightening the sleeve of his t-shirt.

"Wouldn't it be fun to go home next Christmas?" she said. The comment floated awkwardly in the air between them.

Michael stood still, his back toward Mia. Her throat felt scratchy and she wanted to cough, but she needed to appear calm and casual. This was supposed to be a hint, not a death blow to Michael's career. She lifted her mug to her lips and then remembered there was nothing but dregs in it, so she put it on the table.

"Go home? Already?"

"Well, not for good . . . necessarily. Just for Christmas. Our parents would love it, you know. Christmas is still a long way off. I was just thinking we could plan ahead. This last Christmas was so hard, being here in Khartoum and so far away from family."

"Where did this come from, Mia?" Michael turned around and joined her at the kitchen table.

"Maybe I was just thinking about stuff."

"Mia, we came here because we wanted to go to a place where Jesus is not really known. This job at Kellar Hope is really important. What I'm doing improves the lives of those families in the displaced camp. We can't just give up at the first sign of difficulty."

Had Michael not been watching Mia the past six months? Every day was a difficult day. The thought of missing another Christmas was not the first sign of her discontent.

He was right of course. But it made hot tears burn in her eyes. Michael tipped his head to meet her gaze. He placed his strong hand over hers. "We can't go home next Christmas."

Michael left for work, taking Corey to school on the way. Mia spent the first part of the morning playing dolls with Annie and blocks with Dylan. Now the two children were engrossed in a show on TV. Mia eyed the computer. She could price airline tickets to Texas—just to see how much they would cost. That wouldn't hurt anything, would it? Or she could lie on the couch and try to forget these thoughts of leaving.

Mia sighed. She needed to do something worthwhile with her time. She glanced at the TV; the show was near the beginning. She had a good half hour of freedom. What could she do? Mia thought of the guest room. It had never been used for guests and had slowly morphed into a storage space. Maybe she could organize it.

She stood in the doorway of the little room. A daybed lined one wall with a floor-to-ceiling bookshelf against another. On the floor were several boxes full of larger-size children's clothes, toys, and other items that Mia had brought to Sudan but had yet to need. She stacked the boxes neatly in a corner of the room, along with several suitcases.

Once she was able to see the floor, she covered the bed with a clean set of sheets and added a pillow. She spread a small rug on the floor and covered one of the boxes with a flowered tablecloth for a makeshift bedside table. Mia stood back to inspect her work. *Not half bad. This is a nice little guest room. Not that we have any guests.*

Blackness enveloped Mia like a hot blanket. She couldn't see anything. The air was still and stifling. She sensed someone was with her. Right next to her, on her shoulders. What was it? Talons. Like that of a huge bird. They gripped her shoulders and pinned her to the bed. She couldn't move. Terror flooded her veins. Her heart beat wildly.

She tried to take a breath, but her chest felt constricted. Mia tried to scream for Michael, who slept soundly beside her. No sound came from her mouth. *Breathe!* But she couldn't. Something, a presence, sat on top of her. It was killing her. In one final desperate attempt, Mia groaned, "Jesus!" Suddenly, she felt a swishing wind and the brushing of something across her shoulders as the presence flew out the door of the bedroom.

Mia lay frozen in bed. She knew it was the middle of the night. The presence was gone, but terror immobilized her. *A demon.* Fear froze every muscle in her body.

The children! She tried to sit up, but a paralyzing fear made it impossible to move. She should wake Michael. Ask him to pray.

But she didn't. Motionless in the dark, she whispered the name of Jesus over and over again.

The morning sun had already begun to heat up the house when Mia awoke. She flipped on the coffee maker as soon as she rolled out of bed. Peeking into the children's room, Mia felt her shoulders relax when she saw all three children still sleeping soundly. *Thank the Lord!*

She glanced out the glass pane of the front door. A slight breeze tickled the leaves of the lime tree, and a bright yellow bird chirped and hopped about somewhere deep in its branches. Everything looked normal, but Mia didn't feel normal. Her stomach had twisted into a knot and her heart beat too quickly. She tiptoed back to the bedroom. She crawled back in bed and grabbed her Bible from the bedside table.

At the name of Jesus, Satan has to flee. Mia suddenly realized how thankful she was for that tiny bit of air in her lungs that enabled her to speak His name. *Thank You, Lord. Oh, Jesus!* Mia sat in bed, the Bible in her lap, and looked over at Michael. He was just starting to rouse. Should she tell him? She should, but fear gripped her.

"Good morning, Sweetie!" Michael grinned at her sleepily. Mia smiled back. Michael began to move about the room, getting ready for work. Mia randomly opened her Bible to read. She needed a special verse, an assurance. A few minutes later, she closed her Bible and squeezed her eyes shut. *Oh Lord, thank You for saving me last night. Please protect our house, our children, and our family.*

Mia jumped as Michael tapped the door open with his foot. She had not noticed when he left the room. He returned with two mugs of coffee.

"Why so jumpy?" He handed Mia a mug.

"Oh, I just didn't know you'd left the room, that's all." She smiled. "Thanks for the coffee."

"Sure thing. Hey, I don't have to go to the office until later because of the Ramadan schedule."

"OK, that's good. Can you take Corey to school on your way?"

It was just a normal day. Except the scariest thing in her life had happened—and she couldn't bring herself to tell her husband.

❖ CHAPTER 15 ❖

*H*alimah celebrated inwardly that Ramadan was over. She didn't dare let her family see the joy and relief that undoubtedly softened her face. The month of fasting and increased piety in the neighborhood had made her uncomfortable. Abdu pestered her every day to go with him to the mosque. Halimah had given in and joined him after his threat about the song he overheard. She hated every minute of it, but she didn't know what else to do. *I can't afford to be caught by him now — not before I know enough about Jesus to explain it to him.*

The end of Ramadan ushered in the Islamic feast day called *Eid al-Fitr.* Everyone in Halimah's family woke up at dawn to get ready for the day of festivities. In the girls' bedroom, Rania beamed with excitement to wear her new dress.

"Halimah, will you braid my hair and put make-up on me?" she asked.

"Rania! Father will *not* let you leave this house with make-up on!" Halimah laughed. "But I will loan you my gold earrings from last year; they will look nice with your new dress."

Halimah pulled a small, locked case from the wardrobe. The black plastic container held her valuable things. She didn't have much yet, but once she got engaged, she would have a case twice as big, overflowing with large gold medallions and bracelets and earrings and chains. They would be her dowry and inheritance, should her husband ever leave her.

For the time being, Halimah's little black case held three sets of gold earrings, all from her father. Each year he gave the girls money to buy jewelry and clothes for *Eid al-Fitr*. Halimah used to have four sets of earrings, but a few days earlier, she had taken one of the sets to the market and sold the gold.

"I want to buy bigger earrings," she'd lied to Rania who was with her at the time. In reality, she was hoping to give the money to Mansur to buy a commentary on the *Injil*. She hated to lie, but she couldn't let Rania see her desire to learn more about the Christian scriptures.

Rania took the pair of tear drop dangles. Halimah wore the smaller, heart-shaped filigree earrings that were a gift from several years ago. She helped Rania get ready for the day and then put her own new clothes on: a long green skirt and a black blouse. Her new green scarf with tassels on the edges matched perfectly. She would wear it when she left the house later.

Mama looked sophisticated in her pink *tobe* that had blue clusters of flowers printed on it and blue embroidery along the edges. Her large form teetered on blue high-heeled sandals that matched the flowers on her *tobe* and framed the intricate black henna design that outlined her feet. Rows of gold bangles lined her arms and jingled as her hands quickly flew over the kitchen cabinets, arranging colored candies on one tray and date-filled cookies on another. She also filled serving dishes with dried dates and several more varieties of cookies.

Guests would be arriving at the house throughout the day. Rania and Halimah would serve the visitors as they came. But early in the morning, they were free to visit neighbors and wish them "*Kul seni wa entoom taybeen,*" which meant "may you be happy and well all year." Mama planned to join the girls for their visiting and, from the sparkle in her eyes, Halimah knew that she was as excited as Rania.

At seven o'clock Halimah donned her new green scarf and the threesome set out to greet the neighbors. Even at that early hour, groups of people walked along the streets; everyone in new clothes and on their way to visit someone else. Neighbors called and waved and enjoyed a few hours of popping in and out of the houses: eating cookies, drinking sodas, and wishing each other well.

Halimah smiled to see her mother laughing and chatting. The woman seldom left the walls of their home. Halimah knew she was glad for an excuse to do so. Rania showed off her new outfit to her friends, who did the same to her. All the little boys in the neighborhood were dressed in new outfits and had new toy guns and handfuls of tiny firecrackers that they threw at each other's feet, laughing as the pop sent the victim screaming and hopping away from the tiny explosion.

When the women returned home, the men were dressed and ready for the day. Father, Abdu, and Ali were wearing new white *jallabeeyas,* and Father wore a new turban wrapped loftily on top of his head. He was tall like Mama, but his skin was dark, even though he was Arab. Abdu took after him, tall and dark. Ali took after Mama. He was stocky and lighter skinned, as was Rania. They were a handsome family, all dressed in their finest. Were it not for Halimah's wary glances at Abdu and his suspicious staring at her, they might have felt as regal as they looked.

Halimah joined her graduation planning committee on a trip to Tutti Island on the first Friday after *Eid al-Fitr.* The weather was hot, but the sky was blue and the breeze confirmed that it was a great day for a picnic. Ready for an outing after a month of being cooped up, she awoke with a smile and hummed the tune to her favorite praise song, singing the words in her head. *Heaven for eternity! Jesus paid the debt for me....* She would not make the mistake of singing the words aloud again. *There is no punishment or hell for me, and I will live to tell: His blood will cleanse all who believe.*

"Why do you get to go out and I have to stay and clean the house with Mama?" Rania was pouting.

"Rania, you get to be here when Uncle Asim and Aunt Fareeda arrive. You get them all to yourself while I am out."

"No, I don't." Her bottom lip protruded. "Ali will be here and so will Mama."

Halimah resisted the urge to yell at Rania. *I am a new creation in Christ,* she reminded herself. *I need to be kind to Rania instead of harsh.* Halimah took a deep breath, "Rania, you are getting so tall now, just like Mama! If I'm not mistaken, you could probably fit into my clothes. Why don't you pick one of my outfits to wear today."

"Really?" Rania's bottom lip disappeared.

"Really, you can try them on and pick your favorite one."

"Oh, thank you Halimah!" Rania ran to the wardrobe and threw open its doors.

I hope she doesn't choose my purple shirt. She knows it's my favorite. Hmmm . . . Being kind is not easy.

While Rania perused her big sister's clothes, Halimah dressed in a long, denim skirt and a dark blue shirt with red dots that matched the red in the *tarha* she wore. Red tennis shoes finished off her casual attire. She kissed Rania on the cheek and walked out of the bedroom.

"Good morning, Father. May I have some money?" Halimah's father, having just returned from Friday prayers and sermon at the mosque, was relaxing in the *salon* while waiting for her mother to cook lunch. He looked up from a newspaper and smiled at his daughter. He reached into the pocket of his *jallabeeya* and handed her a stack of bills.

"Be careful!" he said.

"Always, Father!" Halimah laughed and headed out the front door. Samia waited for her at the end of the street. Together they walked to the main road to catch a bus to the ferry where the rest of the group would meet them.

The crescent-shaped island of Tutti was only eight square kilometers in size. Tutti boasted one small village and the rest was farm land. The tiny island lay in the confluence of the Blue and White Nile Rivers. Three bustling sister cities that made up Greater Khartoum surrounded Tutti Island, but the little enclave maintained a quiet and rather primitive village life. Tutti's inhabitants, descendants of the Mahas tribe, took pride in their settlement that dated back to the fifteenth century.

"Father said he had heard rumors of plans to build a bridge to connect Tutti Island to the rest of the world," Halimah told Samia, as they made their way from the bus to the ferry dock.

"Yes, my father said the same thing. He says it will never happen because the elders of the island oppose the idea. They say it would destroy their unique culture."

"All I know," Halimah said, "is that the controversy sparks lively debates between Father and Abdu."

The rest of the group was already at the dock when Halimah and Samia arrived.

"Come on! Hurry up!" Jamal called. He was standing knee-deep in the water waving at them with one hand and grabbing the small ferry boat with the other, as if he could keep it from chugging away. The girls laughed and picked their way down the muddy slope to the water's edge. Jamal helped each one wade to the boat and climb in. As he helped Halimah, Jamal whispered in a serious tone, "I need to talk to you."

"What about?"

"Later," he said, then turned and made his way to the other end of the boat, laughing and joking with the other guys.

Jamal was never serious. Why now? And what did it have to do with her?

After a ten-minute ride, the group of friends splashed and laughed their way up the sandy bank of the island. A line of island residents sold candy, snacks, and fruit that were neatly stacked on grain sacks spread across the sand like miniature picnic blankets. Young boys sold bottled drinks out of coolers filled with cool water.

The students climbed the steep bank to a footpath lined by trees with gnarly roots and trunks. As they walked, Halimah peered through the trees and saw simple mud-brick houses and gardens, lots of gardens. Fields of corn rippled in the breeze. Mango and banana trees dotted the edges.

"Khartoum is nothing like this," Halimah said.

"Yea, I feel as if we are walking in a tiny paradise."

Jamal's voice surprised Halimah and she looked around. She hadn't realized the group had walked on ahead, and only she and Jamal were walking slowly, taking in the scenery. Halimah's heart skipped a beat. She looked at Jamal and saw that he was watching her.

"What is it?" Halimah asked, lowering her voice a bit so that the others couldn't hear.

Jamal continued walking a few more steps. Finally, he spoke. "I had a dream."

"OK, we all have dreams, Jamal. What kind of dream?"

"I dreamed about a man in a white *jallabeeya.*"

Halimah laughed. "Well now, that narrows it down, doesn't it?"

"I'm serious, Halimah. It was whiter than I've ever seen."

Halimah saw that Jamal was not joking. He kept walking, his eyes staring at the path in front of them, but he kept talking.

"I asked the man who he was and he replied, 'I am *Isa.*'"

Halimah kept in stride with Jamal, but inside she froze. Why was he telling her this? Did he know about her?

"I said to the man, 'I have read about you in the Qur'an. What do you want me to do?' He said, 'You must go to Souq Isshabi tomorrow and when you see two men approach you, talk to them. They will tell you how to have eternal life.'"

Jamal paused as if waiting for a reaction from Halimah. But Halimah could not speak. Her mouth was as dry as cotton and her mind was suddenly fuzzy. She felt nauseated.

"Lately, I have had problems with my father. Nothing that I do is good enough for him."

Jamal wouldn't stop. Didn't he know that he should stop speaking about this?

"But after that dream I felt so peaceful, Halimah. I felt like I would finally know how to have peace forever."

Could it be? Could someone besides Halimah believe in *Isa?* She ignored the sick feeling in her stomach and forced her dry mouth to speak.

"Did you go to Souq Isshabi?" she asked.

Jamal kicked a stone to the side of the path. "The next day I got ready to go. But then I thought about the two men. Who are they? Are they secret police? Is it a trick somehow? What would they tell me?"

"I think you should go, Jamal. What can it hurt?"

"It can hurt a lot of things, Halimah. Meeting those men could have made my life even more complicated than it already is. It's better just to make the best of things the way they are now. It was just a stupid dream anyway. I shouldn't have told you. It's just that . . . you seem different than the other girls. More serious, or trustworthy, or something." Jamal kicked another stone to the side of the path, a little harder this time. Then he pasted on a giant smile and said, "Beat you to the others!"

Halimah watched Jamal run ahead, but she didn't try to keep up. Her heart sank to her stomach and the fear that gripped her chest melted into sorrow. Jamal was resigned to the turmoil in his life when hope was within reach. It was surely Jesus who had appeared to him. And those men in the market would have been there to tell Jamal how to become a follower. Oh, why hadn't he followed the instructions?

Halimah walked alone until she reached the tip of the island where the rest of the group gathered. They stood in a line, teetering at the top of the four-meter cliff and gazing out over the river. To the left was the White Nile, flowing north from the southern parts of Sudan; to the right was the Blue Nile, flowing north from Ethiopia.

There, at the northern tip of Tutti Island, the two rivers merged into one: the main Nile River that flowed on toward Egypt. The two colors of the rivers remained separate for some distance, before fully combining their different shades of brownish blue. Neither one was truly white or blue.

Halimah kicked off her tennis shoes and began to climb down the muddy drop off. Tree roots emerged from the dirt cliff like spider webs. She easily found footing among the gnarly twists. The other girls squealed at Halimah, and the boys laughed at the jittery girls. But no one joined Halimah. Instead, their heads disappeared from view as they ran to the other side of the narrow tip to find an easier way down.

She continued her descent alone, her bare toes squeezing tightly around the roots that jutted out from the wall of mud. When she made it to the bottom, she found herself standing in knee-high water. The gentle flow of the river tugged at her denim skirt, like a voice beckoning her to come along.

From down below, she couldn't see the merging of the two rivers. All she could see was the brown waters of the Blue Nile. Halimah thought about her decision to follow Jesus. From her own perspective, she couldn't see how it might affect her life in the future—down river, so to speak. All she saw was the muddy water around her. She imagined Jesus up in heaven looking down at her. He could surely see from a different perspective. He could see how all of this would work out. She thought about Jamal and his dream. She thought about Abdu and his threat.

"Jesus, my life is like muddy waters right now. I can't see what is ahead. Please help me learn how to follow you no matter what happens."

There, with the solitude of the river before her, Halimah felt peace.

❖ CHAPTER 16 ❖

Halimah, Samia, and Howeida stepped off the bus in front of Afra Mall, the only mall in Khartoum. Though all three girls preferred shopping at the open markets, Howeida said they should experience this modern version of shopping. She insisted that everyone else in the world shopped at malls.

Howeida led the way toward the two-story building. "We're going to ride the escalators."

"What for?" Samia asked.

"Because Hamid is taking me to Dubai for our honeymoon. There are lots of malls and escalators in Dubai and I don't know how to ride one. I don't want to get there and fall off."

They stopped in the parking lot to buy a drink from a young boy selling water bottles out of a cooler. They stood outside for a few minutes, watching children ride on the kiddie rides and play on a merry-go-round.

"That will be you in about a year, Howeida," Halimah teased, "chasing the first of many little Howeidas and Hamids around a playground."

"*Insha'Allah*," she said, tossing her empty bottle on the ground and walking toward the mall. "It is too hot to ride the bus home. Hamid sent me more money. When we are done here, I'll hire a taxi to take us home."

Samia and Halimah followed, tossing their bottles on the ground as well.

The inside of the building was sweltering. The air-conditioner had apparently broken and Halimah felt as if they had walked into a giant oven rather than a shopping mall. At least the *souqs* were breezy. Something could be said for tradition and open-air shopping.

To the right, they saw what looked like a metal staircase. That, Howeida told them, was the escalator. The metal steps rose smoothly and quickly. What happened to them when they reached the next level was a mystery to Halimah. They seemed to disappear into the floor and new steps appeared at the bottom. The trick would be to step onto the bottom step without falling backward as it moved forward and up.

"We have to act like we know what we are doing, Girls!" Howeida said, "We don't want people to think we have never seen one of these."

"But we haven't!" Samia said, eyeing the machine suspiciously. Howeida glared at her and then marched ahead confidently. She stepped onto the bottom step and simultaneously grabbed the right handrail. Samia and Halimah watched her float upward.

"We can do this," Samia said. She teetered a bit when the stair took off, but Halimah was standing behind her and steadied her as they went. They gripped the moving, rubber railing tightly and glided to the top where Howeida was waiting.

"Now," she said, her voice a little more confident than it had been before, "we go down." The girls followed her up and down a few more times and then decided to stay on the second floor where there was a small food court. Howeida pulled out her money from Hamid and bought each of them a *shawarma* sandwich. They sat at one of the tables that lined the food court. Halimah felt light and free to be sitting in the mall with her girlfriends. *This must be how boys feel all the time.*

"We better get home," Samia said, as she wiped her mouth with the tiny napkin that came with the sandwich, "before my father finds out that we came to the mall and didn't attend a lecture at the university."

"That's what you told him?" Howeida laughed. "You haven't figured out how to be engaged. I just tell my father that Hamid says I can leave the house. Then I call Hamid and tell him that Father says I can leave the house. And there you go: I can do whatever I want. Being engaged is the best time of life. No obligations and no rules!"

Samia rested her elbows on the table, as if contemplating Howeida's advice. Before Samia could give her opinion, Halimah blurted out, "I'm trying not to lie anymore." Samia and Howeida looked at her like she was speaking some Southern-tribe gibberish.

"Ummm, I don't even know what to say to that, Halimah. But, OK. If that's what you want," Samia replied, trying to cover what was becoming an awkward silence.

"Well, I just think that it's better not to lie so much, that's all," Halimah stammered, regretting that she'd said anything at all. "Never mind, let's just go." She straightened her *tarha* over her hair, grabbed her purse, and headed for the escalator.

"No, wait!" Samia called, following after her with Howeida on her heels. "I want to know what you mean. What made you suddenly decide to be concerned about lying?"

"I dunno," Halimah lied.

"Well, what did you tell your father today? I know you didn't tell him you were coming to the mall with us!" Howeida said. She stepped—with almost no hesitation—onto the top step of the down escalator and glided toward the first floor with her friends once again behind her.

"I didn't tell him anything. He wasn't home when I left. Neither was my mother."

"Well," Howeida said, "I'd like to know how you explain your absence to them when you get home . . . and no lying!"

"Leave her alone, Howeida. I think she's serious," Samia said.

Halimah was serious. Suddenly, the electricity went out and the escalator stopped.

"What now?" Samia asked, still holding on to the railing and waiting for the escalator to start up again.

"We just have to walk down like these are normal steps," Howeida said.

"I wonder if this will happen to you on your honeymoon," Samia teased.

Halimah laughed and her friends joined in. She was relieved for the change of subject, but her heart felt heavy at Howeida's words. Her friend posed a valid point. What was Halimah going to tell her parents? More important than that, when was she going to tell them about her new belief? Howeida and Samia obviously noticed Halimah's new behavior. When would she tell them the truth? Her secret was bound to come out eventually.

Could it really be *Eid al-Adha* already? Samia's wedding was just a few weeks away. Halimah mentally counted the weeks, as if she would figure out that everyone was wrong and it was not really the Muslim holiday after all.

"What are you making?" Ali asked, running into the kitchen and peering around Halimah's shoulder to see what she was cutting.

"*Salata aswad,* eggplant dip" she replied, "Mama bought these eggplants from the market, and we need to use them before they go bad."

"How can they *go* bad? They are already black!"

"Well, that just shows that you know nothing about cooking, Silly." Halimah continued to peel off the waxy black skin and then cut the long vegetables into thin round slices, placing them on a tray.

"I don't need to know how to cook, because you and Mama and Rania cook for me and when I am older, I will find a wife to cook for me."

"Well, what if we decide to stop cooking for you? What then?"

"I'll just tell Father and he will make you cook!"

Ali was searching for a big reaction from Halimah, but she refused to give him one. He reached for her wallet that sat on the counter beside her cell phone and *tarha*. Halimah didn't care about the wallet as much as she did about what was inside it. The slip of paper with Mansur's name and number on it was tucked inside one of the pockets.

She would be in trouble if Ali found it. She reached out to try to grab the wallet from Ali, which delighted him. He jumped back and laughed. Then he reached over and grabbed her *tarha* off the counter and ran out the front door waving the *tarha* and the wallet. He knew that Halimah couldn't chase him outside without her head being covered.

You are a brat, Ali! Halimah screamed in her head. But she was not allowed to speak against Ali.

"He's just a boy," Father would say, "let him. He'll learn when he's older."

Fortunately, that had been the truth for Abdu. He had grown up to be a responsible adult who helped Father in the family business. He was also a devout Muslim and tried to be a good and respectable person. Halimah was not sure that Ali would turn out so well. But she didn't say anything to her parents. It wasn't her place.

Halimah forced herself to look calm as she continued to prepare the eggplant. Once he came back inside, she begged Ali to return her wallet. When he realized the fun was over, since she couldn't chase him, Ali returned her things and left to find his neighborhood friends. Halimah peeked in the wallet and saw that he had not taken anything out of it. She breathed a sigh of relief.

She placed a pan on the gas burner and lit the fire. After pouring oil in the pan and letting it heat, she fried the eggplant slices and put them on a plate to cool.

"Ah, your father will be very happy that you are cooking the eggplant dip for him! He says you are an expert at *salata aswad*," Mama said from the doorway.

Halimah eyed her mother with a grin. "Well, I learned from the best."

Mama smiled and sat at the kitchen table. She held an invitation, which she opened and showed Halimah. "It's for Najla Hamoudi's son," she said. "The wedding is Friday."

"Are you going?" Halimah asked, remembering that Najla Hamoudi's family had offended her family last year by not attending her cousin's wedding.

"No! Of course not. I'll send a gift—but a small one."

Forgiveness was hard to come by and never given freely. She was confident that whatever gift Mama sent would be big enough to keep the family reputation spotless, but small enough to remind Najla Hamoudi that she had not forgotten last year.

Halimah dumped the fried eggplant into a bowl and added a thick lump of *dakwa*, Sudanese peanut butter. She mashed the creamed peanuts into the eggplant and added lime juice, pepper, salt, and water. The mixture was blackish brown and smelled strongly of peanuts. Halimah dipped her finger in and tasted the dip. She added a pinch more salt.

"You know what I heard about Najla's family?" Mama asked, obviously in the mood to gossip. "Just before *Eid al-Fitr*, Najla asked her family for money, saying that she needed it for an operation on her foot."

"Yes, I remember that she hurt it badly." Halimah tried to be respectful and not chide her mother for gossiping. But words from the *Injil* rang in her head, "Do not let any unwholesome talk come out of your mouths, but only what is helpful for building others up according to their needs, that it may benefit those who listen." She set the bowl of fresh eggplant dip on the kitchen table and busied herself washing the dishes.

"Well, she did need surgery, and she asked her family for money. I heard that she raised almost the full amount for the operation. But when *Eid al-Fitr* came, she used the money to buy new furniture instead. Can you believe that? Now, she has no money to pay them back, and she still desperately needs the surgery. Her family is furious with her now and won't speak to her."

"What will she do about her foot?" Halimah recalled that before she had become a follower of Jesus, stories like this would have delighted her. Now she just wanted to leave the kitchen and the conversation. But as much as she knew that she should not be gossiping, she also knew that she had to respect her mother.

"Well," her mother replied, "she went to a *sheikh* to see if he could help. He read from the Qur'an and also massaged the foot a bit."

The phone rang and Mama scurried to the *salon* to answer it. Halimah was thankful to be rescued from the gossip session. She was skeptical that Najla's visit to the *sheikh* would do any good. She wanted to tell her mother that Jesus could heal Najla Hamoudi.

Halimah's heart burned with the desire to tell her family about her new beliefs. She hated to keep it from them. But she knew it was too dangerous just yet. Both her parents had quick tempers, and if they learned that their daughter had left Islam, the shame would cause them to become irate.

One day she would tell them anyway, but she wanted to be sure of all that she believed. She wanted to continue to read the *Injil* and the new commentary she had bought. She needed to know more before she was forced to defend her new faith and before her life itself was at risk.

As Halimah dried the dishes and returned them to the cabinet, she resolved that after Samia's wedding in a few weeks, she would tell her family. That would give her enough time. Surely they would understand—if they gave her a chance to explain.

❖ CHAPTER 17 ❖

$\mathcal{M}$ia was glad that Ramadan was over. The strange encounter in her bedroom that night at the beginning of the month had put a creepy feeling in her heart that she couldn't shake. Each day she thought about telling Michael, but how would he react? He didn't even understand her desire to go back home for a visit. What would he think if she told him she believed a demon had attacked her? Would he think she was making the whole thing up?

Mia felt guilty secretly looking for airline tickets from Khartoum to Dallas/Fort Worth on the Internet, but she did it anyway. When Michael was at work, she would look for the cheapest route home. A couple of times she had also done a quick job search to see if there were any openings for work near her parent's home.

With every passing day of Ramadan, Mia had watched in dismay as her heart drifted farther away from Michael. Perhaps now that Ramadan was over, she could shake herself out of the dark cloud she was under.

The day after Ramadan was a Muslim holiday. *Eid al-Fitr*, Michael and Mia were told, was a festive day with lots of visiting.

"Perfect!" Michael said. "We'll be able to go visit Sudanese families together!"

"Perfect," Mia said grumpily.

She hadn't been sleeping well all month and had resorted to tiptoeing to the computer in the living room before it was even light outside. The day of *Eid al-Fitr* was no different. Mia double-checked airline offers to see if any sales had popped up. *Hmmph. There are never sales on flights out of Khartoum.* Then she opened her email program and started to type.

Dear Mom,

How are you and Dad? Michael's job is going well. Life here is definitely an adventure. It is always good to keep options open, so I was wondering if you could check around and see if there are any jobs available for Michael there in his field. You know, just in case this job doesn't work out.

Are you going to be home for Christmas? Wouldn't it be great if we could come home to visit?

Love,

Mia

She looked at the computer screen. She shouldn't hit send. Her mother would read that email and by nightfall the weather man would be announcing a strange whirlwind in Texas. She would be knocking on every door of every company "from here to yonder" to find her son-in-law a job in Dallas.

Mia put her hands in her lap and closed her eyes. She should talk things over with Michael. But things were beyond that now. They were at opposite ends of the spectrum in terms of their opinions about Sudan. She took a deep breath, then opened her eyes and clicked "Send."

The sun brightened the sky and filtered in through the windows of the living room, reminding Mia that it was *Eid al-Fitr*. She woke the children and dressed them in their newest outfits because Michael had learned from the men at the office that most of the Sudanese would be wearing new clothes.

Mia didn't have anything new to wear so she chose the least-wilted outfit she had: a long navy skirt and a long-sleeved green tunic top with embroidery on the neckline. Michael wore a snow-white *jallabeeya*. He emerged from the bedroom while Mia fed the kids toast and jelly.

"Wow, you look good in Sudanese clothes," Mia said, in spite of herself. Maybe she should have purchased a *tobe* like the Sudanese women wore over their clothes. She imagined herself trying to keep the head-to-toe scarf in place all day and decided her skirt and blouse were a better choice.

"Well you look pretty great yourself!" Michael responded. He had been so patient with her during the whole month of Ramadan, even as she grew more and more distant from him. She hated herself for being so moody.

"Thanks." She forced a smile.

As soon as sticky jelly fingers were washed and final bathroom trips were made, the family piled into the Land Rover and headed across town. The first stop would be Abbas' and Widad's house. Michael and Mia began visiting the family soon after Mia and Beth met Abbas on the day Beth gave him a New Testament.

Mia had to admit that she enjoyed their friendship and was so thankful that God had provided a way for her and Michael to share Jesus with them as a family. Abbas had continued to read the New Testament and asked questions about it.

Corey, Annie, and Dylan were always happy to play with little Yusra. Mia was thankful that on this visit, Annie would have a girl to play with. She wasn't so nervous when Annie was around Yusra, like she was when Annie played with the boys at Hanaan's house.

The language barrier between the children was easily overcome by playing with sticks and rocks. Yusra was as cute as a doll in her new frilly yellow dress and yellow hat. She wore Tom-and-Jerry socks and black-patent shoes. She carried a new purse with nothing in it but an old string of dirty plastic beads. Mia brought candy as a gift for the family, so she gave Yusra a few pieces to carry in her purse. Abbas fetched an assortment of sodas from their store and they gave everyone a bottle, even Dylan.

"Where next, Mom?" Corey asked as they waved goodbye.

"Where next, Mommy?" Annie echoed.

"Where?" Dylan mimicked, not to be left out.

"Now we'll go see Dad's friend from work. His name is Mr. Habiib." In spite of herself, Mia was having a good day. Why was it that when she was so frustrated with life in Sudan, she always felt a little better if she spent time with Sudanese? It was counter intuitive and yet true. She even started to regret the email she'd sent her mom that morning.

Habiib and his wife Nahla welcomed the family in generous Sudanese style. They were dressed in fine clothes. Nahla smelled of sandalwood perfume and henna swirled in delicate flower patterns on her hands and feet. She still wore a red *tobe*, which was traditional for a new Sudanese bride. Mia guessed that Nahla was around twenty years old. Habiib looked to be in his late thirties.

It seemed unusual to Mia that Habiib, an Arab, would be working at an aid organization like Kellar Hope Foundation. Most of the problems the refugees in the displaced camps had were at the hands of the Arab government. Michael had explained to her that Habiib didn't actually work for Kellar Hope but had helped them when they needed the local government to grant permission for projects.

Habiib and Nahla lived in a traditional Sudanese-style house. This meant that they shared the property with extended family and that most of the rooms opened into courtyards. In traditional houses, daily chores like cooking or washing clothes took place outside. One room, called a *salon,* was reserved for guests and was furnished with a table and comfortable chairs.

Michael, Mia, and the kids were ushered into such a room. Nahla offered sodas and date-filled cookies to the whole family and loaded the children with candy.

"We are going to have a baby!" Habiib blurted as soon as the two couples were seated in their simple but clean *salon.*

"*Mabrook*, Habiib! Congratulations!" Michael exclaimed.

Mia looked at Nahla who was quiet, but smiling at her husband. Mia mentally counted. Habiib and Nahla were just married five months ago.

"Thank you," Habiib said, beaming. "The first month I thought that Nahla was pregnant, but then she started bleeding and I was very sad."

"*Umhmm*." Mia nodded, trying not to appear mortified that Habiib was talking about something so private.

"Yes, but the next month she did not start bleeding. So we went to the doctor and he said she is pregnant!"

"Oh, that is wonderful, Habiib. I am happy for you," Michael said as he took a swig of soda. Mia smirked and glanced at Michael. He wouldn't look at her. What a hilarious and awkward conversation. Who could have guessed that they would be spending *Eid al-Fitr* eating treats and discussing Nahla's monthly cycle.

Mia could hear the children in the courtyard. They were playing with a kitten and, by the sound of it, were giggling and jumping up and down. They were definitely on a sugar rush.

Later, Mia helped Nahla bring the empty bottles and cookie trays to the kitchen. She watched as Nahla washed the trays. Her skin was dark and smooth. Her eyes, outlined in kohl, were round and deep. Her smile was radiant and she had the slightest dimple in each cheek. She must have made a lovely bride.

Mia was shocked by Habiib's assumption that he would get Nahla pregnant the very first month. Sure, there were lots of honeymoon babies in any country and culture. But to assume it! Habiib was just a tad too prideful in his manliness.

"Will you go home for the birth of the baby?" Mia asked.

"No," Nahla replied, rinsing off a silver tray. "It is customary to go home, especially with your first child. But I told Habiib

I just wanted to stay with him. My family can come visit me at Habiib's house."

"Ah! You are truly in love then," Mia said, smiling. Nahla giggled and dimples appeared on her cheeks. Then her smile faltered just the tiniest bit and she turned to look at Mia.

"So, you have had three babies," she said. "That's nice. Was it easy?"

"Not very easy, Nahla!" Mia answered honestly. "I had to have surgeries all three times."

"But after you gave birth, then what?"

Mia knew that Sudanese women did not read copious amounts of informative material, like Americans tended to do in new situations. Perhaps she really didn't know much at all.

"Well," Mia said, "There's the afterbirth. After the baby you still have to deliver the afterbirth. Is that what you mean?"

"No, not that. I mean after it is all over, that's it for you, right?"

What did she mean?

"I was circumcised, you see," Nahla said. "After I deliver the baby, the doctor will have to sew me back up."

"Ah," Mia said, finally understanding. "For me it was different because I had surgery. But yes, for women in America, they might have a stitch or two if it was a difficult birth, but after the baby is born, it is over."

"Not for me," Nahla said, fear creeping into her voice. "Because of circumcision, the doctor will have to cut me a lot during the birth. Later, I'll have to go back and be sewn up again."

What could Mia say? Should she express sadness over a practice she found to be an outrage? Should she encourage her with meaningless words like "it will all be OK"? Nahla was looking at her as if waiting for an answer.

"Oh, yes that is different," Mia mumbled.

Mia watched Nahla dry the trays. She thought about Nafeesa and her daughters. These girls and women endured horrible pain because of a procedure that could potentially cause additional health problems. But—as with everything Mia observed about women in Sudan—they bore it gracefully and with dignity. They were strong, beyond what Mia would ever have to be.

Annie ran into the kitchen, hands full of candy.

"Mommy! Time to go!"

"Oh, OK. Time to leave, Nahla. Thank you so much. And *mabrook*, congratulations on your baby."

"Thank you, Mia. Come again any time. You are always welcome."

With several more greetings and handshakes and kisses for the children, Michael and Mia herded the kids into the car and headed home. They laughed and talked about the visits. Mia hadn't felt so connected with Michael in a long time. It felt like coming home.

By late afternoon, the Land Rover pulled into the driveway. All three children, now crashing from the sugar high, fell asleep in a sprawled heap on the sofa.

"Want some limeade?" Mia asked.

"I don't think I can have another grain of sugar or I'll throw up!"

"Wow!" Mia laughed. She hadn't laughed in such a long time and it felt good. "How about a tall glass of water?"

"Perfect. I'm changing out of this white dress, and then let's meet on the veranda."

Mia laughed again. She had to admit that it was funny to see her tall, athletic husband wearing a long robe.

Ice water in hand, Michael and Mia settled under the fan on the veranda.

"Michael, something weird happened about a month ago." Mia started talking before she even realized what she was doing.

Somehow their day spent together had softened her. She didn't want to hide things anymore—even bad things. She told about the talons and the choking and how she couldn't breathe. She told about the fear she felt and then how she had been scared to tell anyone.

Michael's face tightened as she talked, but he was quiet until she had finished.

"Has it happened again since then?" he asked.

Mia shook her head.

"We haven't prayed much together lately. I think we need to do that more." Michael's eyes were filled with concern. "I'm sorry you were scared to tell me, Mia. I've been so caught up in work. I've been so concerned with the families in the displaced camps, I guess I kind of overlooked that my own family needs me too."

Michael stood up and took her hand. He pulled her gently from her chair and hugged her. Mia thought she would melt in his embrace. It had been so long since he had held her. This was home—even if it was in Sudan. They could make it work. They had each other. They had the Lord.

"The Bible says that we should 'have nothing to do with the fruitless deeds of darkness, but rather expose them,'" Mia said, though her voice was buried in Michael's arms. "I guess that's probably talking about sin in our lives, but just the same, if I hide something, I am a slave to it. I think that's what happened."

Michael stepped back from Mia and gently lifted her face toward him. "Satan has no right over you, over our family. There is so much evil around us, Mia, but I know that God is stronger."

"Me too. I'm so sorry I've been such a bear this past month. I really do like it here and I want to stay. Today, when we were visiting, I thought that maybe God really does have a plan for us here. I still don't see it. But that doesn't mean it isn't there."

Michael pulled her back into his arms. His embrace told her that all was forgiven. Relief and happiness flooded her veins and she sighed peacefully.

Then she gasped.

"What's wrong?" Michael asked, backing up, his brow wrinkled.

"The email." Mia's voice was barely audible. "I hit *send*."

"What email?" Michael's brow wrinkled.

Mia gulped. Regret tasted bitter.

"An email I shouldn't have written."

❖ CHAPTER 18 ❖

*J*ust as Mia expected, her mother jumped into action when she received the email from her daughter. A quick job search on the Internet and numerous calls around town had produced several tempting job possibilities for Michael. She also shared with her women's Sunday school class Mia's letter, framed as a prayer request of course. Mia wrote several emails over the next few weeks, explaining to her mother the despair she felt in the initial email and the grace God had shown her once she reconciled with Michael.

"Do you think your mother understands now?" Michael asked several weeks later.

"I don't know. I think it's hard for her to comprehend how I could have seemed so desperate and then changed my mind so quickly. I should never have written that email to begin with."

"I think living in Sudan is a growing experience for all of us. Even for your mom. She's being forced to trust God with her daughter!"

"Yea, she thinks we are crazy to be here."

"We are!" Michael laughed. "Now go get dressed or we'll be late."

Eid al-Adha, another Muslim holiday, had arrived. Every Muslim family in Khartoum that could afford it, slaughtered a sheep. Muslims believed that Ishmael, rather than Isaac, was the son God commanded Abraham to sacrifice. In remembrance of the ram that God provided for Abraham in place of his son,

Muslims purchased and slaughtered a sheep. Wealthy Sudanese Arabs could slaughter one sheep for each of their sons.

Habiib invited Michael and Mia to bring their family and spend the day with him and Nahla. She was five months pregnant and her round belly was just beginning to protrude from beneath the folds of her *tobe*.

As Michael steered the Land Rover around potholes and over the bumpy streets, Mia looked out the window at the houses they passed. Sheep had been slaughtered in front of many houses and the blood pooled near the front gates.

As they pulled up to Habiib's house, they saw the skinned carcass of a sheep strung up on the branch of a tree just outside the front gate. A man was cutting off chunks of meat and placing them in a plastic tub. A second plastic tub held the entrails. The sheep head sat at the foot of the tree and stared at the American family as they approached the house.

"*Ahlan wa sahlan!*" Habiib said, as he emerged from the gate with his arms spread wide, "Welcome!"

"*Eid Mubarak!*" Michael greeted his colleague and friend, "Blessed festival!"

"*Eid Mubarak!*" Mia said. And each of the children parroted the greeting, even Dylan.

Habiib laughed heartily.

"*Masha' Allah* they are so smart! *Allah yabarak feek*, Allah's blessing on you, my little friends." He scooped Dylan up in his arms and headed into the front courtyard. "Please! Follow me!"

Mia sat with a group of women on chairs and stools in the open courtyard at the back of Habiib's house. This was the women's courtyard, the cooking area. The indoor part of the kitchen was a small room on the opposite side of the courtyard. A couple of shelves hung on the wall for dishes and a wooden table that held a two-burner gas stove covered one wall. But most of the food preparation seemed to take place outside.

Mia looked around the courtyard. Habiib's mother—called "Mama"—Nahla, and Basima, the wife of Habiib's brother, worked busily. A fourth woman sat on a broken stool in the corner, alone. Her name was Anjel. Nahla introduced her as an afterthought, explaining that she worked for Mama. Mia thought that she must be from the Dinka tribe of South Sudan. Her skin was as dark as charcoal. She was tall and slim, in contrast to her short, plump employer. Anjel appeared to be buck-toothed. Mia remembered an article she read on the Internet about the removal of the bottom front teeth as a rite of passage in the Dinka tribe.

No one talked to Anjel except to fuss at her for not properly washing a plate or for getting in their way. Mia's heart was heavy for Anjel. Did she live with Mama or have a family of her own? Was she a slave?

When the three Arab women chattered and laughed with each other, Mia could not understand them. She was feeling more confident in her Arabic skills, however, and when they talked slowly to her, she was able to understand almost everything they said.

"You don't know how to cook like this, do you, Mia?" Basima asked. Like the other women, she held a sharp knife in her hand and quickly cut chunks of meat off the pile of raw sheep that sat on a tray between them. There were no cutting boards. Blood seeped out of the fresh meat and dripped on the tray. Flies fluttered about, waiting for their chance to descend and eat.

Mia smiled. "No, we do it a little differently."

Nahla's arms jangled with gold bracelets. Except for the beautiful gold jewelry that she and Basima wore, they were dressed casually in floral moo-moo dresses. Since no men were in the back courtyard, the women left their heads uncovered.

As noon approached, people began to show up in the back courtyard. A woman came and then another, and then a small child. Mia could see from their clothing that they were poor. As each one entered the courtyard, Habiib's mother put a handful of meat into a bag and gave it to them.

"This is our Muslim duty," she explained to Mia. "Our family eats one-third of the sheep. We will freeze one-third of it to eat later. We give the last third of it to the poor."

As Mama finished speaking, a small boy walked up to her, his hand held out for meat. She looked him up and down.

"You are the brother of Ahmed and he was just here. I already gave him meat!" Mama's voice was accusatory and loud. The boy turned and ran from the courtyard quickly.

Nahla laughed as she set her knife down and walked over to an outside faucet to wash her hands. "They try to get more meat than their portion. Mama will not let that happen."

Mia glanced at Anjel, who was still sitting alone and being ignored. She wondered if Anjel would get to eat any of the food or if she would be scolded and sent away like the little boy.

Nahla stepped into the little room with the dishes and gas burner. Mia followed out of curiosity. She found Nahla cutting onions and mixing up a paste of hot sauce. Then Nahla began to chop some parts of the sheep that Mia didn't recognize. Perhaps part of it was liver, but there were definitely other organs involved.

"What is this?" Mia pointed to a light pink chunk. Nahla said a word and Mia looked at her in confusion. "I don't know that word."

Nahla smiled and pointed to her throat.

Esophagus? Yuck! Mia thought but asked, "What are you making?"

"*Marara.*"

"Sounds . . . interesting. Do you fry it?"

Nahla laughed. "No! It is raw. You can't fry *marara!*"

Nahla continued to chop the bits of organs and then mixed the bite-sized pieces in a small glass bowl with the sliced onions. Mama came in the kitchen and her eyes danced at the sight of the fresh *marara*. Mia thought about how excited her own mother acted when she made pumpkin pie at Thanksgiving. But wait, that wasn't really the same. What about giblet gravy? Well, at least that got cooked!

Nahla and Mia barely fit comfortably in the tiny kitchen without the addition of Mama's ample body, but she leaned through the doorway and reached over to the bowl of *marara*. In her hand she had some sort of organ from the sheep. Mia thought it was possibly the gall bladder. Mama held it over the chunks of *marara* and squeezed. A yellowish-green liquid dripped over the dish. Mama smiled with satisfaction. Mia fought her gag reflex. She decided most assuredly that she was not going to eat that dish come lunch time.

Basima and Nahla loaded a giant round silver tray with glass plates that held the fried mutton, the *marara*, a chopped vegetable salad, an eggplant dip and long fingers of bread. It was a delectable display of fine Sudanese fare. All except the *marara* made Mia's mouth water. But this tray was for the men.

Nahla wrapped a beautiful red *tobe* around her body and over her head. Then she took the tray from Basima and disappeared through the door that led to the front of the house where the men were seated. Mama urged Mia to follow and join Michael and the men inside.

"Nahla will eat with you in there," she said.

"Really?"

"Oh yes, yes. Now go!" She shooed Mia through the back door. Mia followed behind Nahla through a family room where the kids were. Someone had given them food already. Corey, Annie, and Dylan were happily sitting on the floor with Basima's children and eating from a common tray of fried mutton and bread. All the children, whether brown or white, sported greasy hands and faces as they gnawed busily at the meat.

From there, Mia followed Nahla out into the front courtyard and back indoors to the *salon* where the men sat. The room had upholstered furniture and a coffee table. The pale green walls displayed a variety of wedding pictures of Habiib and Nahla, as well as some black and gold hangings with Qur'anic scriptures written in swirly Arabic script. Habiib immediately ushered Mia to a chair beside Michael and helped Nahla set the heavy tray on the table. Nahla turned to leave.

"Stay and eat with me, Nahla!" Mia called. She just smiled and nodded, saying she'd be back. But, of course, she wouldn't. Mia had been duped. Why didn't she just stay in the back with the women and refuse to join the men? She was an outsider. It didn't seem to matter how hard she tried. She was still not one of them.

She ate quietly and listened to the men's conversation, hoping Habiib wouldn't start talking about Nahla's monthly cycle again.

"If I were president," Habiib said, scooping up a chunk of meat with a torn-off piece of bread, "I would let people choose their religion."

"Really?" Michael asked.

"Oh yes! I would let people decide. People need to have freedom."

"So," Michael said, "if a Muslim wanted to become a Christian . . . he would be free to convert?"

"Oh no!" Habiib said. He looked surprised, almost mortified, as if he had never considered that scenario. "Of course not. A Muslim wouldn't be allowed to convert to Christianity."

"Only a person who wanted to convert to Islam?" Michael asked.

"Right," Habiib replied, satisfied that Michael now understood.

"How is that any different than the way things are now?"

Habiib launched into a lofty explanation that was beyond Mia's knowledge of Arabic. If Michael didn't understand it, he sure faked it well. He nodded and commented at all the appropriate times. Mia watched Michael and her heart beat with pride. He worked so hard to become friends with Arab men like Habiib. He told them about Jesus and prayed faithfully for them. Men like Habiib did not know any Christians besides Michael. *I still don't know what my role is in all of this, but I know I'm here to do something.*

Mia thought about her mother. From the beginning she worried about Mia moving to Sudan and had been horrified that her grandchildren would be raised in a Muslim country. Mia's email had only exacerbated the situation.

"Sudan is not worth your struggles and sadness, dear." Mia's mother had written her. Was that true? On days like today Sudan felt worth it. Mia spent time with Sudanese women. Michael chatted in Arabic. The kids played with other children. *This was a good day. But what about the tough days? Is Sudan worth it then?* Mia wasn't sure.

❖ CHAPTER 19 ❖

*H*alimah felt ready to pop, like a spring pressed into a tiny box. Mansur had invited her to attend a Christian conference. Finally, a chance to learn more about her new beliefs. The timing was perfect. The conference was held each day after her classes at the university. Halimah could attend and her parents would think that she was studying with Samia or meeting with the graduation planning committee.

Ugh! It's the first day and I'm already late leaving campus. Halimah walked quickly toward the giant metal gates that secured the university. Her heart sank when Jamal caught up with her.

"Hey Halimah! Where are you going? Aren't you meeting us under the tree today?"

"Me? No . . . I have stuff to do."

"Since when do you have stuff to do?" Halimah quickened her pace, but Jamal matched his steps to hers. "Something is going on, I can tell. I've seen you reading that book, by the way. That black one."

"Book?" Halimah swallowed hard. Lately, she had been hiding a small book in her purse to read between classes.

"Yes, book! Is that a Christian book, Halimah? I don't care if it is, I just want to know."

"It's the *Injil*, Jamal." *There—I said it. I'm not going to lie.*

"Please, don't tell your father. He will kill you, Halimah, you know that. You will bring shame to your family, and he won't have a choice. Listen, I don't care what you believe, but I don't want you to get hurt or killed."

"Well, thank you for caring, Jamal." Halimah kept her dogged pace toward the gate.

Jamal stopped and she felt him watching her leave.

"Just be careful, Halimah. Don't do anything stupid," he called.

Halimah stopped and turned around. Her gaze shifted to the hundreds of students walking about campus behind him. They didn't know what would happen to them on Judgment Day. Halimah's heart tightened. She felt sorry for them. None of them had hope. Only Halimah did.

"I haven't done anything stupid, Jamal. I've made the smartest choice of my life."

Halimah turned back around and walked out of the gate.

The conference took place at a retreat center surrounded by fields of wild grass and small acacia trees. In the distance, the Nile River meandered calmly down a path toward Egypt. The late afternoon sky was blue like the sea and the breeze off the water disguised the oppressive heat.

When Halimah arrived, the meeting had already begun with singing and clapping. Someone played a small drum and a young woman stood at the front, singing into a microphone. Halimah saw lots of Southerners, their black skin giving them away. She didn't see any Arabs.

Why would you, Halimah? Arabs don't believe in Jesus. Maybe this wasn't such a good idea. She was definitely out of place.

But before she could change her mind, Mansur appeared out of the sea of dark skin and walked toward her, smiling. Halimah smiled back. He greeted Halimah with a handshake and motioned for her to follow him. He led her through the crowd to where his family sat. A tall man stood next to them. He was a *khawadja,* a white man. Halimah tried not to stare.

The first speaker taught about what it meant to be a disciple of Jesus. Halimah recalled reading the words of Jesus in Luke 14:26–27. Jesus said, "If anyone comes to me and does not hate his father and mother, his wife and children, his brothers and sisters—yes, even his own life—he cannot be my disciple. And anyone who does not carry his cross and follow me cannot be my disciple." But the speaker taught that Scripture also said believers should pray and fast and study Scripture and tell others this good news. Discipleship was like growing in knowledge of and faithfulness to God, through Jesus.

I want to be a disciple.

The words of the speakers from the conference echoed in Halimah's head as she slipped into bed that night. She wanted to quietly ponder the teaching, but Rania was in the mood to talk.

"Mama says that Najla's family doesn't have enough money to pay for the club that they rented for the wedding on Friday. Mama says that Najla is asking neighbors for money and that everyone is getting frustrated with her and that . . . "

Halimah feigned attention, but really she was thinking about the conference. Up until that point, she had been reading the *Injil* and thinking about what it said. But at the conference Halimah learned a simple way to actually study the Holy Book. After reading a section of Scripture, she could ask herself questions like: Is there a promise to claim or a commandment to obey? What lesson is taught? What questions do I have about this? What can I change in my life to obey this passage?

Halimah could hardly wait to try it out, but Rania was still talking, "and then Mama told her that she should go tell the other women in the neighborhood and then no one will give money and then . . . "

Pulling the sheet over her head she whispered, "Rania, please stop!"

Halimah tried to pay attention during lectures at the university, but accounting didn't interest her anymore. She sat at the back of the lecture room and absently drew henna designs on the corner of her notebook. A grin crept across her face as she thought about the conference. The first day had gone so well. Her parents had not said anything about her late return.

Today was shaping up to work out just as well. Halimah's father planned to spend a few days with a holy man at a mosque in the desert. He was traveling with two friends and the *sheikh* from the neighborhood mosque. *Haboba* was visiting and her mother would be distracted by a houseguest as well as the latest neighborhood drama: the Najla Hamoudi family wedding.

She glanced at her watch. Maybe the teacher would let them out early. All she wanted to do was study the Bible. Halimah had received a copy of the entire Bible at the conference and she was eager to read the stories of all the prophets. She was familiar with some of them, as the Qur'an spoke of the same ones. But there were other prophets she had never heard of.

In addition to the new Bible, Halimah had used her *Eid* money to buy a commentary. She had hidden these new treasures in the wardrobe along with her *Injil*. Halimah's heart thumped a little faster as she imagined the stack of books that grew under her pile of clothes. It was getting crowded in there. In fact, Mansur had given her a very small copy of a book called *John* and she had decided to hide that one under her mattress. She was going to have to start finding other hiding places as well, if she continued collecting books.

In between lectures, Halimah and Samia left campus to get some guava juice at a nearby café. Halimah felt a tug in her heart, something that prompted her to tell Samia about her secret. After purchasing the drinks, the girls sat at a little metal table inside the café.

"Samia," Halimah said, "you know that we've been friends for a long time. You've trusted me with even your deepest secret."

"Yes, Halimah, of course I do. You're my best friend."

"Well, I have a secret of my own. It won't be secret for long though because I want to tell others. But I want to start with you." Halimah paused and looked around the café. She adjusted her *tarha* so that it stretched more tightly around her head. She looked her childhood friend in the eye. "I did not fast during Ramadan."

Samia jerked her head a bit in surpise. "Really? That's your secret?" She stirred her guava juice with a straw and watched the thick swirls. "Well, don't tell your father. And you'll have to make it up."

"No, that's not all of it, Samia. There's more." Halimah lowered her voice. "I am a follower of Jesus."

Silence.

Halimah looked at Samia. Her face did not show anger or even surprise. Samia looked like she was at an outright loss for words. She opened her mouth a couple of times, but no words came out. Finally, she said, "What do you mean?"

This moment was what Halimah's heart had been waiting for. She had the chance to share with her best friend about the most awesome news she had ever heard. Eternal life was not about doing good things or fasting or eating the right foods or even wearing the right clothes. It wasn't about maintaining family honor. There was no condemnation in Christ Jesus. There was no difference between Arabs and others. Everyone was meant to have salvation as a free gift. It was almost too good to be true . . . almost. But Halimah knew it was true, and she felt her heart overflow as she told Samia.

When Halimah finished, Samia pressed her lips shut and looked at her with quizzical eyes as if to ask, "Could this be true?"

When she finally spoke, though, a glint of hardness glossed her eyes. "It sounds good, Halimah. But we are Muslim, we can't follow Jesus."

"Samia, that's what I mean, it's not about what religion we are born into. It's about God making a way through Jesus. It's about forgiveness. *Forgiveness*, Samia! Forgiveness for all I've done. Forgiveness, Samia, for all you have done!"

Samia's eyes filled with tears. "I would like to be forgiven."

"Samia, you can be!"

"But Halimah, you will be killed! I know your family. Surely you have not forgotten. Your father is well known for being a very good Muslim, as is your brother, Abdu. Your family name is spotless."

"But don't you see? None of that matters if I have the Truth." Halimah leaned over the table toward her friend. "It is the Truth, Samia! I have no doubt in my mind."

"Halimah, I am happy that you have forgiveness. I will not tell your secret. But I am not brave like you. I never have been. I cannot do what you are doing."

"It's not about being brave, Samia!"

"Yes, Halimah, it is. I cannot risk changing my life, just when things are starting to go right." Samia's eyes looked sad. The friends finished their juice in silence. When they stood to leave, Samia grabbed Halimah's hand, "I will not tell your secret," she said.

Halimah could not answer. There was a knot in her throat. But it was a broken heart that prevented her words. She thought for sure that the Truth would be obvious to her friend. If she couldn't convince her best friend, how would she convince her family?

❖ CHAPTER 20 ❖

*H*alimah enjoyed the second afternoon of the conference even more than the first. Surrounded by other believers, her spirit floated like the water birds gliding over the nearby Nile. Halimah joined her voice with others, and they blended together in beautiful Arabic praise songs to God. They sang of His love and His patience. They sang of His gift of salvation.

Halimah never sang beautiful praise songs in Islam. She had learned to recite *suras* in a chanting way. The words of the *suras* were poetic, but she never felt her heart and emotions truly touched as she did at the conference.

After the sessions were over, Halimah left quickly. She wanted to return home in plenty of time to help Mama cook dinner.

"I will come again tomorrow," she promised Mansur and his wife as she headed to the street to find a rickshaw.

When Halimah walked in the front door of her house, she knew that something was wrong. Her father and Abdu were standing in the *salon* looking at her with somber faces. What was her father doing home? He should have been out where the holy man lived by now. Mama and *Haboba* were standing behind them. Rania and Ali were nowhere to be seen. Abdu was the first to speak, and his voice was deep and tense.

"What are these, Halimah?" He stepped to the side and Halimah gasped. There on the floor behind him was her *Injil* and her Bible commentary. Halimah stared at the books.

I'm not ready for this. I need more time to learn, to prepare my defense.

"Halimah, are you a Christian?" Abdu's words broke the silence. They forced themselves from his mouth through gritted teeth.

Words from the *Injil* (Luke 12:8–9) flooded Halimah's head: *I tell you, whoever acknowledges me before men, the Son of Man will also acknowledge him before the angels of God. But he who disowns me before men will be disowned before the angels of God.*

"Yes, I am," Halimah replied, lifting her eyes from the books on the floor to the eyes of her older brother. In that moment, that moment of confessing Jesus as her Lord, Halimah's heart was overcome with peace. Confidence pulsed through her veins. At the same moment, Halimah's father wailed a strange guttural howl of grief. He stepped forward and slapped Halimah across her face. She stumbled and tasted blood in her mouth.

As she regained her balance, Halimah saw her father raise his other hand. He held a large kitchen knife. Halimah remembered Jamal's warning. She knew that her father would kill her. She had shamed the family—tainted their good name. Her death was really the only way to preserve her father's honor. And honor was all he had.

Halimah closed her eyes but did not flinch. She'd known that this day would come. But before his hand swept down upon her chest, *Haboba* grabbed his arm from behind. Her physical strength was not enough to stop the strong arm of a shamed man, but her place of honor in the family kept him from thrusting the knife.

"Stop!" *Haboba* cried. "Don't kill her, my son! If you want to use the knife on her, then cut off her hair."

Abdu stepped forward and yanked the *tarha* off Halimah's head and her father roughly grabbed her long hair that was held at the nape of her neck with a rubber band. The men cut her hair raggedly against her scalp.

Father gave *Haboba* the knife and the two men pushed Halimah into her bedroom. Over the next hours, until the evening prayer, the men questioned Halimah about the books and about who she was meeting with to learn about Christianity. No matter what answer Halimah gave them, they hit her.

Halimah felt sorry for her father and brother. She knew they were scared. Her father slapped her across the face with his palm. But Abdu had a wooden broom and he hit her on her side and back. *What else can they do?* They continued to question her, but the more they hit her, the less coherent her answers seemed.

Her thoughts retreated deep inside her. She was not afraid, and somehow she didn't feel pain. But she was dizzy and her vision began to blur.

"Halimah, *habeebtee*, you don't really believe in Jesus. Just say the *shihada,* and we will pretend this never happened," her father pleaded.

"I cannot do that, Father," she said through split, bloodied lips. "Jesus is the true way to God. I cannot deny the Truth."

He slapped her again. The room spun around her head.

When the *muezzin* called the faithful to prayer at eight o'clock, Abdu and Father grabbed Halimah by the arms and forced her into the bathroom in the back courtyard.

"We can wash her there, like *wudhu.* Maybe that will get rid of the evil spirit in her," her father told Abdu.

Halimah didn't fight, but when they were done and all three stood, fully clothed and dripping wet in the courtyard, she spoke. "You can wash me, but I will not stop believing in Jesus."

"You have brought dishonor to our family, Halimah," her father screamed. He wiped his hands dramatically against each other, as if brushing off dirt. "You are no longer my daughter.

I disown you. We have never had a Christian in our family, and we will not begin today!"

Mama and *Haboba* were watching from the doorway. They were crying and hugging each other. Halimah's father stormed past them.

"She is possessed by a spirit," he said, "and we must rid the spirit from our house. Take her clothes and belongings and burn them."

The women did as he said. They took every piece of clothing and every pair of shoes that Halimah owned. They took away her black case with the gold earrings. Mama made Halimah change into an old dress that she used for cleaning the house so that she could burn the soggy clothes that Halimah wore.

Halimah sat on her bed. She tried to lie down to rest, but she could hear the yelling and crying of her family outside the door. Oh how she wanted to go out and comfort them. But that was impossible. She was the reason for their misery.

Sometime in the middle of the night the door flew open. Halimah's father and Abdu marched in again.

"Halimah, say you have not really turned from Islam. Say that there is no god but Allah and Mohammed is his prophet." Abdu was begging this time.

Halimah looked him in the eye. "I cannot."

Somewhere in the confusion of the beatings and the yelling, Halimah realized that Rania and Ali had returned home. Where had they been? Perhaps Mama sent them to a neighbor's house. Her father called Rania and Ali into the bedroom. He looked at them and gestured toward Halimah, a bruised woman in a raggedy dress.

"This girl is no longer my daughter, and she is no longer your sister. Rania, you are my only daughter now." Rania began to cry, and that was the first true pain that Halimah felt during the whole evening. It stabbed her heart like the knife was meant to do.

Sleep evaded the house that night. Halimah was locked in her room alone. She tried to lie down, but her side and legs were aching and her head was throbbing. She sat on the edge of her bed and tried to remember Scripture verses. She quietly sang the praise songs, finally free to sing them in the house because she no longer had a secret.

The last beating was just before dawn, when Abdu and Father tried one more time to force Halimah to say the *shihada*. Halimah found it hard to speak with her mouth as swollen as it was, but she managed to force her lips to form words.

"I believe that Jesus is the Son of God."

"Then we will not speak again," her father said quietly and they left the room. They did not lock the door, however, and a few minutes later Rania came in. She looked scared and her eyes were red and puffy. Halimah sat on the edge of her bed, but Rania did not come to her as she would have done in the past. She stood across the room just inside the door, as if she wasn't sure what to do or think.

"It's OK," Halimah said. "Rania, come here, just a little closer."

She took a few steps toward her big sister.

"Rania," Halimah whispered, "you have to understand, what I believe about Jesus is true. I want you to know that Father does not have all my books. A small book called 'John' is hidden under my mattress. Later, I want you to read it. It will tell you the truth, Rania. No matter what happens, remember it will tell you the truth."

Rania whimpered and fresh tears ran down her cheeks. "I don't want you to go."

"What do you mean, Rania?" Halimah asked, and Rania looked back toward the door. Halimah limped to the door and cracked it open. The voices of her father and Abdu drifted in from the *salon*. They were talking about stoning her. Halimah knew this was a legal action in Islam. Then she heard her father suggest the *khalwa* that he had been planning to visit—the one he was supposed to have gone to. Halimah's shoulders tensed. This was the same thing her uncle had done to Bashir.

Halimah closed the door carefully and glanced at Rania. The young girl looked sad and scared. Halimah felt a sudden and urgent prompting that she thought surely must have come from the Holy Spirit—she had to leave. But how could she? She had no *tarha*, no clothes, no shoes and nowhere to go.

"Rania, do you have any money?"

Rania did not ask why. She went to her part of the wardrobe, took some money from her purse, and handed it to Halimah.

"Rania, don't worry about me. Jesus is taking care of me. Remember, you must get that book that is hidden and read it. It is the best news you will ever read about."

With that, Halimah opened the door quietly and peeked out. She could hear her mother in the kitchen cooking breakfast. She could see Abdu and her father in the *salon*. Their backs were turned toward her. Halimah took a deep breath and walked down the hallway toward the front door. She opened it.

The men in the *salon* did not turn around. Mama did not stop cooking. Rania did not say a word from where she stood in the bedroom. Halimah did not know where *Haboba* or Ali were, perhaps asleep. What she did know was that she was in the middle of a miracle. She simply walked out of her house with no one noticing.

Halimah walked quickly down the empty street. Even at an early hour, people usually walked the streets of the neighborhood, but that morning the street was empty. She glanced tentatively behind her. No one followed her. She could hardly believe it. There she was: a battered girl walking down the street barefoot, wearing a torn dress and no *tarha*. How far could she get . . . really?

❖ CHAPTER 21 ❖

As Halimah stumbled down the quiet street of her neighborhood, she could make out, in the early morning haze, a rickshaw coming toward her.

It's another miracle. Halimah felt like a little girl whose daddy kept giving her presents. Halimah did not recall ever seeing a rickshaw driving down her street. The road was not paved and had too many holes and big rocks for a rickshaw. She raised her hand limply and hailed the three-wheeled vehicle. The driver, a young dark-skinned teenager, stopped the vehicle and stared at Halimah, not even attempting to hide his surprise at her pitiful appearance.

"Get in," he said, turning his gaze to stare out the front windshield.

"Really?" Halimah asked.

"Just get in," the driver said again, with urgency this time. He glanced up and down the street while Halimah ordered her sore body to climb into the rattling contraption.

The engine, what there was of it, revved and the wheels propelled them forward. The driver turned the motor-cycle type handle bars sharply so that they made a U-turn and then headed in the direction Halimah had been walking. Halimah relaxed a little when the front gate of her house was out of sight.

"Where do you want to go?" the driver asked. Halimah was sure that the poor kid had about twenty other questions he would have preferred to ask. It was better for him not to know. Where *did* she want to go? She didn't know. She couldn't go to Samia's house, or any of her friends for that matter. She was an infidel now. No Muslim would help her.

Then Halimah remembered Omar and Lana. She met the couple at the conference, just the day before. They were from the Nuba Mountains but lived in Khartoum. She had been surprised to learn that they lived only ten minutes away from her. She leaned forward and gave instructions to the driver.

"I don't have enough money," Halimah yelled to the driver over the rumbling of the rickshaw motor. "Just get me as far as you can," she said, telling him how much money she had. The teen nodded and kept his gaze straight ahead.

Halimah tried to keep her head down and prayed that no one she knew would see her. There she was: a girl in Sudan with no family, no money, no phone, and no identity papers.

I am nothing. But I have Jesus, and that is enough.

The rickshaw driver took Halimah all the way to the house she had described. When he stopped, she slid down from the back seat and handed him the money.

"I know it is not enough. I am sorry," she said. She tried to smile, but winced instead.

"No," the driver said. Then he revved his engine and puttered away without looking back.

Halimah's head was spinning and, this time, not because she had been slapped. She walked up to a blue metal door that was screwed into a dirty white wall. This couple was obviously not as well off as her family. Halimah swallowed the lump in her throat and the pride in her heart and knocked on the door. She needed to get out of the street as quickly as possible because she looked like a beggar or a crazy woman and, if anyone saw her, news would spread.

A few seconds later, the gate opened and the woman Halimah recognized from the conference peered out. Shock came over Lana's face as she recognized the young Arab woman.

"Halimah! *Salaam Aleykuum.* Come in, quickly." She opened the gate wide and let Halimah in. Looking around to see if anyone had been watching, she quickly closed the gate.

The dirt *hosh* that the women were standing in was small. Two metal beds were still set up from the night, and Omar was taking down the bamboo poles that held up the mosquito nets over the beds. He greeted Halimah cheerily until he stepped closer and saw her face. His hands, which had been holding the poles, dropped to his sides, and the poles clattered to the ground around him.

"Halimah! What happened?"

"They found out, didn't they?" Lana asked. She took Halimah's hand and guided the battered girl to one of the beds. "Sit here." She patted the mattress. Halimah meekly obeyed, happy to have someone else make the decisions for a while.

It looked as if the couple had been fixing their morning tea. An aluminum charcoal stove sat on the ground with a pot of tea bubbling on top of the glowing bits of charcoal. Omar fixed Halimah a cup of tea while Lana gathered a bucket of water and a bar of soap to wash Halimah's face. Halimah hardly spoke to the couple. She felt as if they understood things that Halimah didn't even know how to explain. Had they experienced something similar themselves? If they had, it would have been at the hands of Arabs: Halimah's own people.

When Halimah finished a cup of tea and washed her face and arms with the bucket of water, the wife gave her a clean set of clothes to wear and a *tarha* to cover her head. The clothes were too big for her, but anything was better than the old housedress she had been wearing. Halimah emerged from the little room where she changed her clothes and saw that Lana was pouring a second round of hot tea. Tea sounded good to her. She had not eaten or had a drink since leaving the university the day before. Halimah sat down on the bed, across from the couple, who sat on the adjacent bed.

"We should pray," said Omar. "And then we need to call Mansur. He will know what to do. It is not safe for you to be here."

Lana nodded. "Your father is a well-known man. He will have many people helping him search for you."

Halimah knew they were right. She bowed her head and prayed along with the couple. When they were done, Omar called Mansur.

"Our new sister has run into some trouble."

How strange to not be referred to by her own name. Halimah had just lost everything she owned. Would she now lose her name too?

"It is not safe for her to stay here," Omar was saying. "It is too close to her father's house."

Halimah agreed. Eventually someone would find out that she was here.

"When did they call? What did you say? All right, we'll continue to pray." The man ended his conversation and turned to Halimah. "Your father has your cell phone and has already called Mansur and probably every other number on your phone."

"But I didn't put Mansur's number on my phone!" Halimah said.

"He probably looked at your call log."

"Oh. I never thought to erase the log." Halimah was glad she had not decided to go to Samia's house. Her friend would not have been able to lie to Halimah's father. Of that she was sure. It was better for Samia if Halimah did not speak to her again. A tear trickled down Halimah's cheek.

"It's OK, *habeebtee*." Lana moved closer to Halimah and patted her shoulder. "The Lord will take care of this. We can trust Him."

Can we? I've never had to trust anyone with my life before. And here I am, trusting two Nuba Mountain people and the Lord, all of whom I've only just met.

Wednesday morning was busier than usual for Mia. Michael had been invited to attend a spiritual conference with a Sudanese man whom he'd met at the international church they attended. He had already attended two days of meetings and was eager to attend a third. Mia agreed to take Corey to school all week so that Michael could go to work early. As she buckled the children in the car and drove to the school, Mia tried to remain positive.

It is a great opportunity for Michael to get to participate in this conference. He'll probably get to meet some members of an underground church. But the crazy voice in her head was just as vocal as the positive one. *Why does Michael get to go to the conference while I have to stay home with the kids? I'm the one who has read books about persecution and underground churches. I think he should stay home with the kids and I should go.*

Mia's head reeled at the mental argument going on all morning as she half-heartedly played with Annie and Dylan. By the time the children were down for their afternoon nap, she was exhausted. She fell to her knees right there in the kitchen where she was washing dishes.

"Lord," she prayed, "I'm so tired of listening to the lies in my head. I trust You. I know You have things under control. I know You have a plan for me. Help me to quit struggling and trust Your plan."

The phone rang just as a warm sense of peace was lifting Mia's heart. She rose from her knees and dashed to the living room.

"Mia, this is Michael. I need you to send an email out to our church friends back home. Ask them to pray for a young woman who is in a lot of trouble."

"What's wrong?" She remembered Michael mentioning that he had met an Arab girl who was a new believer.

"The family of that girl I told you about found out she has become a follower of Jesus. They have beaten her, and Mansur thinks they will try to kill her."

"OK, I'll send an email out now." She paused. "Hey, if she needs a place to rest, she can come here."

"I'll tell Mansur," Michael replied.

"All right, Honey, 'bye."

Mia hung up the phone and sent an email to their family and friends who she knew would pray.

Dear Friends,

Today we are asking for your earnest prayer for a sister in Christ in the country where we live. Her life is in danger because of her new faith. We ask that you pray for her protection, but even more importantly, that you pray for her faith to remain strong. I'm sorry that we cannot give you more details. But when you pray, rest assured that the Lord knows all the details and He is in control. Hebrews 10:33 says, "Sometimes you were publicly exposed to insult and persecution; at other times you stood side by side with those who were so treated." Let's stand side by side with this new sister.

Thank you! Michael and Mia

Mia read over the email. She had often read about persecution, but she had never experienced it in such close proximity. Suddenly, her own problems seemed very small.

An hour later, Michael called Mia again. "Mansur and the other house church leaders talked and they decided to bring the girl over to our house so she can rest. She has been up all night and is exhausted. They think our house will be the safest place for her right now since her father is already searching for her."

"I'll get a bed ready for her," Mia said. Her heart beat wildly. She was the benchwarmer who had finally been called into the game.

Perfect timing! Mia thought as she remembered that she had just cleaned up the spare room. She put fresh sheets on the bed and fluffed the pillows. If this girl had been beaten, she would need a lot of rest. Mia felt honored that God would let her play a part in standing side by side with a persecuted believer.

Mansur called Omar and asked to speak to Halimah. "Your father will not think to look for you in the home of a *khawadja*," he said. "You will be safe there until we can find a place for you to live or until your father's anger subsides."

Even as he said the words, Halimah knew the latter would not happen. Her father would never live peacefully with someone who brought dishonor on the family. Halimah was not safe as long as she was within his reach.

Mia looked across the *salon* at Halimah. She wore an ill-fitting shirt and jeans with a belt cinched tightly to hold them in place. Her hair was wrapped tightly in a red scarf. Her face was swollen. After introductions, they sat awkwardly for a few minutes. Mercifully, Mansur broke the silence. "Omar and Lana live not far from Halimah's house. She went to their house when she left her family, but it is not safe for her there."

"We are honored to help," Mia replied. "Halimah is welcome to rest here until you decide what to do. I have a bed ready for her. Let me get you some tea," Mia stood to go to the kitchen.

"It's better if I leave quickly," the pastor said, as he stood. He nodded at Halimah. "You will be safe here. We will contact you later. God be with you."

When Mansur was gone, Mia turned to Halimah. What did one say to a girl who had given up everything to follow Christ? The books she read did not tell her that. She knelt beside the chair where Halimah sat and placed her hand over the girl's.

"I love you, my sister," Mia stumbled through the Arabic words. "And you will be safe here. Let me pray for you. But ..." Mia laughed. "I may have to use some English words too. My Arabic is not so good."

"It is OK. I understand," Halimah said softly in English.

Halimah appeared to be sleeping soundly in the guest room. Mia tried to go about her day as usual. But it was difficult knowing that—according to the law—she was harboring a criminal. Mia's thoughts were interrupted by the sounds of Annie and Dylan waking up from their naps.

What on earth was she going to tell the children?

❖ CHAPTER 22 ❖

*H*alimah lay on the bed in the loneliness of a dark and quiet room. She had never slept alone before. Rania or *Haboba* or Samia, or even Mama had slept in the same room. She was never just alone.

Halimah touched her face. Her mouth and jaw ached. Her right eye felt as if needles were poking into it repeatedly. She closed her eyes and listened to the gentle rattle of the ceiling fan. She was exhausted from the night's events and the morning escape and did not argue when Mia left the room, though she wished the kind woman would have stayed. She closed her eyes and drifted back into a deep sleep.

Dylan toddled directly into the kitchen. "Snack please!" He called, opening the fridge and peering inside. Mia settled him at the dining table with a cup of juice and some bread.

Michael arrived at two o'clock after having picked up Corey from school. The decibel level in the house rose exponentially. What was it with boys and noise? Annie could play quietly with her dolls, but if the two boys were added to the mix, the games became loud. If imaginary guns weren't shooting, then a race was on; if no competitions were taking place, then wild animals were roaring; and if wildlife was absent, then motors were revving and cars were honking. She was thankful that the kids played well together and, as soon as Corey's backpack was unpacked, the threesome was deep into an imaginary game outside.

"Where is she?" Michael asked, looking about from where he stood, just inside the front door.

"She's sleeping," Mia said, nodding toward the guest room.

"Mansur said they would leave her here a day or two until they find a place for her."

"That's fine. She can stay as long as she needs."

"They tried to kill her."

"Who would do that?"

"Her family. Her father wanted to stone her."

How could a father want to kill his own daughter? Did he truly love her? The words registered while their meaning eluded her: a father stoning a daughter. What did it matter that she had different beliefs? Was he really willing to murder his daughter just because she chose to leave Islam?

"How did she get away?" Mia asked.

"Mansur wasn't sure. He just received a call from Omar and Lana after Halimah arrived at their house. That's when I called you. She has no place to go where she will be safe. We are sure that her father has notified the police and all the checkpoints leading out of town. He's an important man; he knows people."

"Well, he doesn't know us," Mia said, surprised at the defiance in her voice. "She can stay here."

Halimah didn't wake up all afternoon. Michael returned to the spiritual conference. By the time he returned that evening, the girl was still asleep.

"She is breathing," Mia told him. "I peeked in to check."

After dinner, Mia helped the children get their baths and then the family sat in the living room together to pray before bed.

"Tonight we have a very special prayer request," Michael said. "We have a visitor with us."

"Really? Where?" Corey asked, looking around the room.

"Well, she's asleep in the guest room," Mia said.

"Does she have jet lag?" Annie asked. She was the logical one of the bunch.

"No," Michael replied, "she had a very hard time last night, and she is very tired."

"When you meet her tomorrow," Mia added, "you will see that she doesn't feel well. She believes in Jesus, but her family does not and they are very angry with her."

"Are they Muslim?" Corey asked.

"Yes, they are," Mia answered.

"Did her family hurt her?" Annie wondered.

"Yes," Michael said, "they did hurt her. They don't understand, yet, about the love of Jesus for them."

What a strange conversation. How could they make persecution child-friendly?

"Is she alive?" Dylan asked, as if he sensed the need to participate, but was unsure how.

"Yes, Honey." Mia pulled the toddler onto her lap. "She is alive."

"She was hit by some people in her family," Michael said, "but she's going to be OK. But since our guest is very special, we have very special rules. We cannot tell anyone about her. She needs a secret place to rest, and we can help her get well if we keep her a secret."

"That's a big secret!" Corey said.

"Yea, a really big secret," Annie said, holding her arms out wide.

"Big secret!" Dylan squeeled.

Oh dear, is this really going to work?

Mia slept on the couch that night. Halimah had fallen asleep without any painkillers, and Mia worried that she wouldn't sleep through the night. At midnight Mia heard the creak of the guestroom door and saw Halimah's form appear in the doorway.

"Hello, Halimah," Mia sat up. "How are you feeling?"

"Kind of in pain ..." Halimah still looked drained.

Mia pointed to the coffee table and said in Arabic, "Look, I have an Arabic Bible and a notebook for you. Mansur said you loved to study the Bible."

Halimah's eyes brightened. "*Shukran,*" she said. "I do."

After showing her where the bathroom was and determining that she didn't want food, Mia brought her a glass of water and some pills to ease her pain. Halimah took them, picked up the Bible and notebook, and returned to her room.

Mia fell asleep again on the couch but awoke with a start when she heard the faint squeak of the guestroom door again. Her neck and back felt stiff. She stretched and looked out the window. The morning sun was beginning to shine and Mia guessed it was around six or six-thirty. She had tossed and turned all night, listening for Halimah, but she must have fallen asleep in the wee hours of the morning. Halimah appeared in the doorway and then walked slowly to a chair near the couch and sat gingerly, favoring her right side and leg.

"You slept well?" Mia asked.

"Yes, thank you."

Mia noticed that Halimah's face was particularly swollen on one side and the white of her right eye was blood red.

"You must be hurting," Mia said. "Let me get you something to drink and some medicine for the pain."

Halimah nodded a thank you and sat quietly.

Mia returned from the kitchen a few minutes later with a cup of water, a mug of hot tea with milk and sugar, and some bread. Halimah immediately drank some water and obediently swallowed the pills for her pain. She had taken the scarf off her head and Mia noticed her wiry hair was cut short and unevenly.

Leaning toward the coffee table, Halimah picked up the mug of tea, but when she took a sip she winced and set the mug back down on its tray. She took a drink of water instead.

"So, what happened, Halimah?" Mia asked. She knew the question was abrupt, but she wasn't concerned with cultural niceties. "How did you get away?"

Halimah began to tell her story and Mia listened, horrified and fascinated at the same time. She thought about the book on persecution that she had been reading. She kept it on her nightstand. Halimah's story was just like that—only it was really happening.

When Halimah finished the story, she seemed drained again. Mia guessed that talking about it had been hard, both emotionally and physically.

"I think you need to rest some more, Halimah," Mia said.

Halimah did not protest. She rose again and walked slowly back to the guest room.

❧ ❦

While Halimah slept, Mia cooked breakfast for Michael and the kids and helped Corey get ready for school. At seven-thirty Corey was ready to go, but he was not happy that he had not yet met Halimah.

"Why is she still sleeping, Mom?" he asked.

"She has been through a lot, Corey. We have to give her time to rest. You'll get to see her later. Do you remember what we said about our special guest?"

"It's a big secret!" Annie yelled from the dining table.

Mia ignored Annie and tried to ignore the panic that rose in her chest.

"Mom, don't worry, I won't say anything," Corey said.

When did my little boy grow up? Mia wondered. He sounded so mature.

Michael grinned and gave Mia a quick kiss.

"I'll be back after the conference tonight."

"OK, see you then. Thanks for taking Corey to school."

"Of course," Michael replied. "We don't want to leave Halimah alone."

With that, he shooed Corey out the door and the two left in the Land Rover.

As usual, Mia opened the gate and then shut it when the car was out. This time, before shutting the gate completely, she stepped out just far enough to glance up and down the street. Life was going along as normal. To the left was Hanaan's house and further down the street was a bushy growth of bougainvillea. The purple and fuchsia flowers of the unruly plant spilled over a neighbor's wall, adding lively color to the otherwise dusty street.

To the right, about 100 yards away was a police station. Mia could see a guard standing at his post near the entrance. Had they received a notice from Halimah's father that his daughter was missing? Had they noticed anything unusual going on? Would they come to ask questions? They would surely be surprised to know that a criminal was right there in the *khawadja's* house, just a stone's throw away.

"Lord, please keep Halimah safe," Mia whispered as she shut the gate.

❖ CHAPTER 23 ❖

As Halimah slept into the morning, Mia sprang into action. First, she rummaged through her stash of medicines and found ointments and a new bottle of aspirin that Halimah could keep in her room.

Next, she made a list of the things that Halimah needed: clothes, toiletries, shoes. Mia thought about Halimah's hair. The locks had been cut off up against her scalp. Mia knew that hair extensions were sold in the market. She wondered if she could figure out how to weave them into Halimah's short patches. Maybe Halimah could tell her how. She added "hair extensions" to the list.

"Watcha doin', Mommy?" Little Dylan came up to Mia holding a toy car in each hand.

"Well, hello there, Little Guy!" Mia picked him up and set him in her lap at the dining table. "I'm adding some things to my shopping list."

"Can I make one?" he asked.

"Well sure, Honey, let me get you a paper." Mia set him on the floor and got a piece from the computer printer in the living room. When she returned, Dylan was gone. Mia heard the squeak of the door to the guest room. It was too late to stop him. Dylan had already gone into Halimah's room and was talking to her.

Mia was setting the table for lunch when Halimah and Dylan emerged from the bedroom. Halimah smiled. It was the first smile Mia had seen from the girl since she arrived.

"Hello! How did you sleep, Halimah?"

"I slept well, thank you." She walked to the dining table holding Dylan's hand.

"I made stew for lunch. You are probably really hungry. Let's eat!" Mia set the pot of warm beef stew on the table.

"Annie!" Mia called. "Time to eat!"

Annie came out of the kids' bedroom holding a doll in her arms. When she saw Halimah, she stopped and stared.

"It's her!" she said, like Halimah was Santa Claus or the Tooth Fairy.

"*Shhh!*" Dylan said, wrinkling his brow and putting his finger to his lips. "It's a secret!"

Though Michael and Mia agreed not to tell anyone about Halimah, they decided to share their secret with Beth since she was a nurse. That evening, Beth came to the house to meet Halimah and do a triage. She looked at Halimah's eye, felt her jaw, and looked in her mouth with a flashlight. When Beth examined her side, Halimah winced and yelped. Her mocha skin hid the severity of the bruises, but Mia saw that her thigh and her side and back were discolored. When Beth was finished, Mia walked her to her car.

"She was beaten badly, Mia. From what I can tell of how deep the bruises are, it is a miracle that Halimah has no broken bones or internal damage. I'm also amazed that the only broken skin is in her mouth and on her lips. We can thank the Lord for that. Just ask her to take pain medication and rest and eat well. As for her eye, I'm not a professional on that, but the blows to her head were severe enough to have caused damage that could be permanent. I know you don't want anyone to know she's here, but I would still recommend that she see an ophthalmologist to rule out a detached retina or other injury. She says that her vision is blurry and her eye hurts a great deal. So an eye doctor is my recommendation."

"Michael and I will talk about it. Thanks for your help, Beth. Just pray, OK?"

"I'd like to help buy whatever things Halimah might need," Beth said. "I don't have to work tomorrow. I'll buy the stuff and bring it by and see if you guys need anything else."

"Sure, I actually have a list right here." Mia pulled out the wadded list that she had crammed into her pocket at lunch time. Halimah had requested a few items, including a hair pick and lotion. "Thanks, Beth. This is a big help. I don't really want to leave her alone at the house. I worry that someone will find her here."

"It's my pleasure. See you tomorrow!" Beth hopped into her Land Cruiser and with a wave of her hand drove away.

"What are we going to do?" Mia asked Michael that night.

"I'll do some checking around tomorrow to find a hospital with an ophthalmologist," Michael said. "We'll just pray that we can get Halimah in to see a doctor and then back out again before anyone recognizes her."

"What do you think, Halimah?"

Halimah was sitting on the couch watching an American sitcom. She looked up at her hosts. "I think I need to see a doctor. I think we should try."

"All right then," Mia said. "We'll do it. I'll call Beth to see if she can stay with the kids tomorrow afternoon."

Beth arrived early on Friday afternoon and brought with her a brand new duffel bag bulging with goodies.

"These are for you, Halimah. You'll find some new clothes in there as well as the other things you asked for."

Halimah's eyes grew wide as she took the bag and unzipped it to inspect the contents. "Oh, thank you so much!"

Halimah emerged a few minutes later wearing new clothes. Beth had done a great job at guessing her size. Mia thought that Halimah looked gorgeous in a new cotton shirt and long denim skirt. She had covered her head in a green scarf and wore a pair of large sunglasses.

"Perfect, Halimah," Mia said. "Just keep your head down and let Michael do the talking and we'll be fine." Then she turned to Beth. "Pray for us!"

Mia and Halimah sat in the back of the car while Michael drove. It was Mia's first time out of the house since Halimah arrived two days earlier. She stared out the window watching the normalness of life going on. But it looked different this time, or was she different? *I'm hiding a runaway girl.* Not a spoiled teen who didn't like her family but rather a runaway who loved her family dearly, but was running for her life.

Halimah sat quietly, her sunglasses hiding her eyes and her scarf covering everything on her head except her face. When the threesome pulled up to the side of the hospital, Halimah gasped.

"This is near to where my cousin works." Her voice was even and flat. Was she nervous? Mia couldn't tell. But they had come this far, they had to go on with the plan. Michael went into the hospital first to make sure the opthamologist was there. Halimah and Mia sat in the back of the car frozen, as if no one would see them if they sat still. A few minutes later, Michael returned and said the doctor was in and was able to see her.

The women got out of the car and walked straight into the hospital, following Michael as he led them past the entryway and up two flights of stairs to a waiting room. If climbing the steps was painful for Halimah, she didn't show it. Adrenaline must have overcome any discomfort because she walked briskly. Mia walked right beside her, trying to stay between Halimah and anyone who walked near them.

The waiting room was a small area filled with rows of plastic chairs facing a counter. The walls were painted white but smudged with a thousand dirty handprints that blended into giant brown smears. Two staff members worked behind the counter and a handful of patients waited in the plastic chairs.

Michael pointed them to the back row in the corner by a window and they quickly sat down. Halimah, with her sunglasses still on, looked down at the floor. Mia scoured the room. She felt as if they had entered the enemy's lair. *How ironic that we are trying to receive treatment from a Muslim for an injury caused by a Muslim.*

No one gave a second look. Mia relaxed. Michael stood at the counter and talked with one of the staff, a young man in a white coat and glasses. After a minute or two, Michael walked back to where the women sat and told them it was time to see the doctor.

They walked past the counter, following the young man in the lab coat to a room. He knocked on the door, and when a voice inside answered, the staff member opened the door. The doctor inside was an Arab man in his mid-forties. He was neatly groomed and looked very classy in his stylish glasses and Western clothes worn under a pristine white lab coat.

His office looked more like a businessman's workplace than a doctor's office. No diplomas or certificates hung on the walls, just a few posters with giant eyeballs and some reading charts. Mia knew that most doctors had a private practice, but regulations also required them to work at public hospitals as part of their service to the country. Perhaps that was the reason no personal credentials were on the walls; it was a shared office. He stepped around from behind his desk and shook hands with Michael. He motioned for the group to sit down in the chairs on the other side of his desk.

"Salaam Aleykum. I am Dr. Fareed. Let me take a look." Remaining very businesslike, he began examining Halimah's eye. He asked her to look left and then right, up and then down. He looked into her eye and touched the skin around it. When she winced, Mia winced too. She wished she could somehow experience the pain in place of Halimah, but instead she sat helplessly.

"She has been hit very hard, which could have caused damage to her eye." Dr. Fareed looked at Michael and then Mia. "She should have come in sooner."

Was that an accusatory tone that Mia heard in his voice? She wanted to retort, *"Well, Muslim men shouldn't beat their daughters!"* Even as she thought it, she realized that Halimah loved the people who beat her and still hoped they would come to the Truth. Mia knew that she too must love the people. They were deceived. Who but deceived people would think it was honorable to beat another human being, a fellow creation of God?

Suddenly, Mia realized that the doctor might assume it was Michael or Mia who had hit Halimah. Mia's mouth was dry and she couldn't form any words. It seemed odd that he did not ask why she had been hit; he simply asked why they didn't bring her in when it first happened. Mia was both relieved and then horrified at all that implied. Her thoughts were interrupted when Michael answered the awkward question.

"We didn't know where to go. We have only just now been able to find a doctor."

"Well," replied the doctor, "she could have had permanent damage, but she doesn't. The blood behind the eye should clear up in a couple of weeks. I will write a prescription for a cream to put on her eye twice a day, and her vision should return to normal." He took out a prescription pad and began to fill it out. Pausing, he looked at Halimah. "What is your name?"

Halimah froze.

"Just give any name," the doctor said.

Again, Mia was shocked. Did this happen so often that the doctor wasn't surprised at her reticence? Were beatings common enough that this doctor would accept Halimah's anonimity so willingly? Did he see a lot of daughters beaten by their fathers? Or wives beaten by their husbands?

Halimah answered with a combination of common names in Sudan. "Samira . . . Najeeb."

The doctor scribbled the name on a prescription form and handed it to Michael.

"You can give her aspirin for the pain," the doctor instructed Michael. To Halimah he said, "*Ya'ateeki al-afeeya*, Allah give you health."

That night as Mia drifted off to sleep, she thought about the events of the day. In Texas a new believer like Halimah would be attending the New Members Sunday School class at church. In Sudan Halimah was also going through a discipleship program—a much more intense one. Mia whispered a prayer of thanks for their safety during their trip to the hospital. Surely Halimah's faith in the Lord had been increased that day.

❖ CHAPTER 24 ❖

"What are these for?" Halimah asked as she walked out of her room. She was holding up three bags of hair extensions.

"For you!" Mia said with a grin.

"Who is going to fix my hair?" Halimah asked.

"Me!"

"You?" Halimah threw her head back in laughter. "You are going to braid my hair?"

"Sure!" Mia said. "How hard can it be? I braid Annie's hair all the time."

"Annie's hair is silky and soft!" Halimah said. "It is nothing like my hair!"

"Oh, come on, we can do it. You can tell me how and I will do it."

Halimah shook her head and giggled. "Well, we can try."

"We can do it now. How long will it take?"

"A couple of hours if you are fast."

"Really? Two hours? How can it take that long? It's just braids."

"It will take at least a couple of hours. That's how long it took my *haboba* and she was an expert."

"All right, if you say so. Bring me your comb; we might as well get started."

At Halimah's instruction, Mia clipped large portions of hair to the side and pulled out tiny sections at a time. The hardest part was at the nape of Halimah's neck, where the hair had been raggedly cut close to her scalp. She pulled and tugged to get enough hair to hold the extensions tight as she braided.

Halimah's hair was rough and kinky. The wiry curls tangled in Mia's fingers, making her work difficult. After half an hour of work, Mia's fingers ached. She leaned back against the sofa. Her back hurt from sitting hunched over Halimah's head. She surveyed her work and groaned.

"Only four braids? That's all I've done?"

Halimah laughed. "It will get faster once you get the hang of it. I can help once you finish the back. I can do the top and sides."

"How long will these braids last once we get them in?" Mia asked.

"Several weeks. I will put some cream in my hair. And I won't wash it much. That will make my hair break and mess up the braids."

"Well, I hope they last several months," Mia said. "This is hard work!"

Mia spent another hour on Halimah's braids. When she finished, Halimah had long black braids that hung down past her shoulders.

"It's beautiful, Mommy!" Annie exclaimed. She had been watching the project in fascination.

"What's wrong with her hair, Mom?" Corey asked. He was staring at the sides and top of Halimah's head. The unbraided portions of her hair were no longer clipped back and now spread out into an afro all around her face.

"Don't worry," Halimah said, laughing. "I am going to braid the rest of it myself."

"I'm sure you can finish it much faster than I can," Mia said, rubbing her aching fingers together. Half an hour later, Halimah emerged from the bathroom where she'd been looking in the mirror to finish the job. The top and sides of her hair were braided in small corn rows away from her face and the braids of natural hair neatly blended with the braids of synthetic hair in the back. She looked stunning.

"Mommy," Annie said, when she saw Halimah. "Miss Halimah looks like a princess! Can you do that to my hair?"

Mia groaned. "I don't think my fingers can take any more braiding, Annie." She fluffed Annie's soft blonde curls, "and I don't think your hair would look like Miss Halimah's."

"Well, she is beautiful." Annie grabbed Halimah's hand and gazed up at her new long hair, smiling.

❦

"Will you read the Bible with me?" Halimah asked Mia one morning.

"Of course." Mia smiled. "I'd love to. Let me get my Arabic-English Bible."

"I was thinking we could read First Peter. You can help me with English and I can help you with Arabic."

Bibles in hand, the two women sat on the couch in the living room. Michael was at work, Corey at school, and the two young ones were playing with toys on the floor. A week had passed with no solution for Halimah. Mansur had informed Michael that her family grew more and more desperate, wondering where she was. Her father had been scouring her neighborhood and had questioned Omar and Lana. Mia couldn't help but wonder if Halimah's family would eventually find her. What would happen if the police showed up at the gate? Mia wasn't prepared for what might transpire.

"In his great mercy he has given us new birth into a living hope through the resurrection of Jesus Christ from the dead, and into an inheritance that can never perish, spoil or fade—kept in heaven for you," Mia read the words in Arabic, slowly and carefully. She wondered what Halimah was thinking. An inheritance kept in heaven for Halimah. This must be a very special promise for a young woman who had lost everything she owned.

Halimah continued the passage: "who through faith are shielded by God's power until the coming of the salvation that is ready to be revealed in the last time. In this you greatly rejoice, though now for a little while you may have had to suffer grief in all kinds of trials."

Suffer grief indeed! "These have come so that your faith—of greater worth than gold, which perishes even though refined by fire—may be proved genuine and may result in praise, glory and honor when Jesus Christ is revealed." Mia finished reading the chapter and smiled at Halimah. "Your faith is being proved genuine!"

A shadow crept across Halimah's face.

"What's wrong?" Mia studied the wrinkles on Halimah's forehead.

"I don't know exactly. My heart is not at rest."

Mia watched her friend flip through the pages of her Bible. *Lord, it would be comforting to receive some sort of sign of affirmation that You are still in control of this situation.*

"Come on, Halimah, let's go make some coffee." Mia grabbed Halimah's hand, coaxing her into the kitchen. Mia preferred drip coffee with lots of milk. Halimah preferred instant coffee with spoonfuls of milk powder and sugar. Mia laughed, "Instant coffee is supposed to be quick, Halimah. That's why it's called *instant*. You take ten minutes to make instant coffee!"

Usually Halimah's eyes sparkled at any humor, and she would throw her head back and laugh. That day, though, she remained solemn. She stirred the liquid in her steaming mug, watching the creamy brown swirls.

"I want to fast for three days."

"Halimah, I know that fasting is taught in the Bible. But your body is not fully recovered from the beating." Even as the words left her lips, Mia felt ashamed. Who was she to discourage Halimah from doing what she felt the Holy Spirit had impressed her to do? "Well, please at least drink water during the day and eat at night. If you do that, you can fast, but also honor God by taking care of your body."

"Yes." She nodded. "Maybe I will do that."

Halimah had taken to spending her afternoons and evenings watching American shows on television. Too much godless media, Mia felt, but what else was Halimah going to do with her time? After sharing a cup of coffee, however, Halimah spent the rest of the day praying and reading her Bible. She disappeared into her bedroom and shut the door. Mia could hear the steady hum of Halimah's voice as she poured out her heart to God. Mia watched in amazement as her friend diligently fasted and prayed for three days. *Could I be that dedicated?*

On the third evening, Michael went to a coffee shop to meet Mansur and Omar. This was their first meeting since the day Mansur brought Halimah to the house. They met in a distant part of town so as not to draw attention. The kids were in bed and Halimah and Mia sat in the living room reading their Bibles and talking about fasting.

"I will finish my fast tonight," Halimah informed Mia.

"And how do you feel now?" Mia asked.

"Peaceful," she replied.

Just then the gate creaked open and a few moments later, the Land Rover rumbled into the driveway. Michael was home.

"*Salaam aleykum,*" he said as he walked into the living room and plopped into an empty chair.

"How did it go?" Mia asked.

"Mansur and Omar think it is a good idea for Halimah to call her family on the phone."

"Why?" Mia asked. "That sounds dangerous."

"Well, the rumor around her neighborhood is that her family thinks she committed suicide and they are in a panic."

"I thought her father wanted to stone her?"

"Stoning me would bring back their honor. But suicide is different. It's shameful." Halimah's voice made Mia jump. Sometimes she forgot that she and Michael were not the only adults in her house anymore.

Michael turned to Halimah. "They are still searching everywhere for you. Your father keeps calling every number in your cell phone's contacts list to try to find you. Mansur thinks that if your family can hear your voice, maybe they will calm down."

"Yes," Halimah said, "this is a good idea. This is what we need to do. Now I understand why the Holy Spirit wanted me to fast. I needed to prepare for this. When should I call?"

"Tonight," Michael replied.

"Tonight?" Mia squeaked, jumping to her feet. "That's a little sudden, don't you think? I mean, this is gonna be dangerous right? Can't they find her if she uses a phone? Can't they track her?"

Halimah touched Mia's hand and looked up into her eyes. "It's OK. This is what I need to do. I am ready."

"Mansur has gone to the market to buy you a *tobe* to wear over your clothes," Michael said. "Omar will take you far away from here in his work car. There you will find a public phone shop to make a short call. You can just tell your family you are fine, but you are not coming back home."

"I'm going to get dressed so that I'm ready when they come," Halimah said.

Mia turned to Michael. She wanted to be strong and confident like Halimah, but her heart was drowning in fear. Was this really a good idea?

"Don't worry, Mia." Michael reached over and grabbed her hand. "These men are wise. They know what they are doing. And God is in control."

Mia watched as Halimah, covered from head to toe in a new *tobe*, got into the car, and sped away. She wanted her mother to begin praying in earnest and pass along the prayer request to church members, so she sat down and typed a quick email. When she was done, she plopped down on the couch and tried to send up her own prayers, but she couldn't focus. How long would it take Halimah to make a phone call and return? When should she start to be concerned that there might be a problem?

"God is in control." Lord, is this your sign?

❖ CHAPTER 25 ❖

*O*mar drove the shiny black car into the darkness. Halimah sat in the backseat, adjusting her *tobe* close around her face. She was not used to wearing a *tobe* since she was not a married woman. But she had seen her mother put one on every day for as long as she could remember. For a fleeting moment, Halimah wondered if she would ever wear a *tobe* for a reason other than hiding her identity.

Those thoughts quickly disappeared as she strained to get a look at the scenery around her. It was dark and she couldn't see much. It was better that way because if she could not see much, maybe she would not be seen either.

"How are you doing, Halimah?" Omar asked from the driver's seat.

"I am doing well, thank you," she replied.

"Lana and I are praying for you every day."

Halimah thought about Omar and Lana, and about Mansur, and the wonderful *khawadja* family she was living with. All of them were risking their own safety to help her. Halimah had not experienced this kind of love in Islam, even within her own family. She hadn't known love like this even existed.

Omar drove for a long time and the later it got, the dustier it got outside. A dust storm was blowing in from the surrounding desert. Once in the outskirts of the city, Omar pulled over to the side of the road next to a large truck that appeared to be hauling bags of onions. The driver of the truck must have stopped on the side of the road to rest for the night.

"You will see a store with a phone just on the other side of the truck," Omar said.

"*Tayib*," Halimah said, "good." She swallowed, hoping that would somehow suppress her fear of being caught. "Lord, be my strength," she whispered as she forced herself to open the door and get out.

The dust blew around her, and she grabbed the edge of her *tobe* to keep it tight around her head. As she rounded the parked vehicle she realized that, because of the truck and the dust, it would be unclear to anyone in the store where she had come from. As far as they could see, Halimah emerged out of the dust like some sort of apparition.

As she walked into the little shop, a single light bulb blinded her eyes. She squinted at the man behind the desk. Clutching the money Omar had given her for the phone call, she asked to use the phone and the young man pointed her toward a table with a phone.

Halimah was thankful to see that the makeshift booth was in the back of the store and the men who were in the store were chatting and laughing quite loudly at the front. She quickly dialed the number for her house. The phone rang . . . once . . . twice . . . three times.

"*Salaam aleykum*." Halimah heard the deep voice of her mother.

"Mama."

"Halimah! Halimah! It's you! *Alhamdullillah*! *Ya* Rania, *ya* Rania! It is your sister, she's alive! Oh Halimah, how are you? We thought you were gone forever."

"Mama, you have to listen to me."

"Here is Rania; she wants to hear your voice. Speak to her!" Halimah could hear Mama crying and saying "*Alhamdullilah*" over and over in the background as Rania took the receiver.

"Halimah?" Rania's voice was tentative, as if she didn't really believe her mother.

"Rania, it's me, Halimah."

"Oh, Halimah! I am so glad to hear you! Please come back!"

"Rania, are you doing OK? How is everyone?"

"Everyone is OK, Halimah. Please come home!"

"Rania, I need to talk to Mama." This was getting nowhere and Halimah needed to get off the phone before they found a way to figure out where she was. Rania gave the receiver back to Mama.

"Halimah, please wait, I am sending Rania to get your father. He is down the street. I want you to talk to him."

"Mama, I can't wait for him. I love you all, but I am not coming home. Please don't look for me anymore."

"But Halimah, just wait for your father."

"Mama, tell Father that I love him and tell him I am OK. I want you to stop looking for me. I am not coming home."

Halimah took a deep breath and, with all the self-control she could muster, placed the receiver back on the phone. *Click!* Halimah willed her mind to ignore her broken heart. She paid the man at the desk and disappeared into the dust, rounding the onion truck and jumping into the black car that waited for her on the side of the road.

"Go!" she said quietly to Omar.

Before anyone could even think twice about the stranger who used the phone, the car had disappeared into the night.

That night Halimah lay awake in bed. Why did Michael and Mia make her sleep by herself? American customs were so strange. After what seemed like hours of trying to fall asleep, Halimah took the mattress off her bed and dragged it into the children's room. She put it down on the floor just inside the door of the room and lay on it.

Dylan stirred in his bed and Halimah lay very still, hoping he would go back to sleep. She peered into the darkness and saw his little form come over to her bed. He stood beside her mattress, watching her. Was he scared? Did he wonder if she was a ghost? After a few seconds of quiet observation, he squatted down, looked Halimah right in the face, and grinned really big. Then he crawled onto her mattress and fell asleep.

Halimah felt her body relax. She looked at his curled up body and thought of Rania. She was much older than Dylan, of course, but she often crawled into bed with Halimah at night. Who was sleeping in her room with Rania now that Halimah was gone? Rania would never sleep there alone. Perhaps *Haboba* slept in Halimah's bed on those first days that she was gone.

What about the book that was hidden under her mattress? Had Rania found it? Did she read it? Halimah desperately hoped that Rania would not get caught with it. What had become of her collection of books that her father and Abdu found in the wardrobe? Her father respected holy books. He would not dare to burn them or throw them away, even if they were Christian books. Perhaps someone from her family would take the time to read them.

Her thoughts shifted to Samia. Her wedding would be any day now. She had almost completed all the beauty preparations for the wedding and had been diligently studying the dances for the *subhia*, the bride's dance party. Her family had been trying to secure a reservation at one of two different clubs. By now they had surely reserved one.

Halimah was supposed to be in the wedding party. She had been Samia's best friend for years, after all. She should be buying a dress and discussing the program with Samia. Yet here she was, lying on the floor with a little *khawadja* child asleep in her bed, with no plan for what to do next.

Oh Jesus, I am giving up a lot for my belief in You. But You gave up even more still. I can never repay You for all You did to give me hope and peace. I trust You!

Dylan twitched and rolled over, tucking his legs up under him so that his bottom stuck up in the air. Halimah remembered when Ali used to sleep like that. He had been such a cute little boy, just like Dylan. Her heart tightened in her chest and tears surprised her. They came like a flash flood, filling up her eyes and rolling down her cheeks. How she missed her family! Her heart ached from the pain. They loved her; she knew it. But, in their eyes, what she had done was deeper than the love of family. She had taken away their honor.

They don't understand yet, Lord, Halimah said in her heart. Was she talking to herself or to Jesus? She wasn't sure. *Hiding in this khawadja family's house is crazy. I hide all day when I should be with my family, finishing my studies, helping Samia with her wedding, sleeping near Rania so she won't be alone. Who will speak up for my cousin Bashir if not me? Maybe I should just go home. Let them beat me. Let them send me to the* khalwa. *I can make it. You will give me strength, Lord!*

Halimah rolled on her back and stared into the darkness above her. She remembered what Mansur had said to her just before arriving at Michael and Mia's house on that fateful day: "Don't try to go back home, Halimah. Your father is very angry with you right now and nothing you can say or do will change that. You are no longer safe. In my experience it will be five to seven years before you are safe to go home."

Yes, Lord, I hear You. I will not go home. I will stay here and trust You. I know You have a reason for me to be here. Please give me strength to be patient. I think being patient and hiding is harder for me than being beaten. But You are worth it, Jesus. Whatever You ask me to do, I will do it.

❖ CHAPTER 26 ❖

A month passed. A month filled with hours of talking and laughing. A month of prayers and tears. A month of jumping each time the doorbell buzzed or the phone rang. Who was it and were they looking for Halimah? It had been a month of rearranged schedules and lives turned upside down.

Mia and Michael agreed that Michael should never be home alone with Halimah. They knew that in Halimah's conservative Muslim family it was inappropriate to be alone with a non-relative of the opposite gender. They wanted to make Halimah feel as comfortable as possible. This, of course, meant that Mia could never leave the house unless Michael was with her or unless Michael was already gone.

They also agreed that, for Halimah's safety, they would not invite people to their house. If anyone came unexpectedly, Halimah went to her room and waited until the guest was gone. Sometimes Mansur came, but even he tried to meet Michael at an outside location. He did not want anyone following him to the house. They all knew that in Sudan, it was not unusual to be followed by secret police or by someone who had been paid to spy.

Mia knew that Halimah's family might still be searching for her. Whenever she heard the doorbell ring, her heart skipped a beat. She automatically bent down to look between the bottom of the gate and the ground to see what sort of shoes the visitor wore. Army boots might imply a police officer.

She wondered if she should go ahead and think of what she would say if a policeman were to come to the gate and ask to search the house, or ask if Halimah was there. But when she prayed about it, she felt a definite answer from the Holy Spirit that came in the form of a Bible verse, Matthew 10:19–20. "But when they arrest you, do not worry about what to say or how to say it. At that time you will be given what to say, for it will not be you speaking, but the Spirit of your Father speaking through you."

One evening, just after eight o'clock, there was a knock at the gate. Mia's heart pounded. She looked at the bottom of the gate. Two sets of feet and the hems of the clothing looked as if it might be a man in a *jallabeeya* and a woman in a *tobe*. What if Halimah's family had found the house? Who else could it be at this hour? Mia stood frozen in the doorway, staring at the gate. Michael patted her on the shoulder.

"Go tell Halimah to hide," he said, as he headed across the front yard toward the gate.

Mia dashed back into the house to find Halimah. She was taking a shower. The water was running and Mia could hear her singing softly. Everything happened in a matter of seconds and Mia only had time to knock on the bathroom door and tell Halimah that Sudanese were coming into the house. Mia wasn't even sure Halimah heard the warning.

As Mia returned to the front door, she saw that the guests were Abbas and Widad, along with little Yusra. Mia tried to make her heart feel happy and flattered that they would come all the way over to her side of town to make a visit. She forced herself to smile and welcome the guests into the *salon*. She couldn't help but think about how the living room was situated between the bathroom and Halimah's bedroom.

"*Salaam aleykum!*" Abbas said as he entered the *salon*, followed by Widad and Yusra and finally Michael.

"*Aleykum wassalaam!*" Mia smiled a little too brightly and shook his hand. "'*Utfudulu!*" She gestured for them to sit down.

The first few minutes were spent exchanging the normal chit chat. Michael slid into his role as host naturally and kept up the conversation while Mia continued to fight panic on the inside and tried not to look distracted on the outside. After a few minutes, she slipped out to the kitchen to get glasses of water for everyone. She filled the gold-colored kettle with filtered water, plopped a couple of cinnamon sticks and cardamom pods in, and set it on the stove top. Then she took the tray of water glasses to the *salon* for the guests.

"Where are your children?" Abbas asked.

"They are already sleeping," Michael replied.

"Sleeping? So early?" Widad was incredulous.

Mia smiled and nodded, trying her best to hide her annoyance. *This is not early. Little children need their sleep to be healthy.*

"Ha ha!" Abbas laughed. "*Khawadjas* have such funny habits!"

It was no use trying to explain. Mia gave up and went to the kitchen to get the tea. As she returned, rounding the corner and heading to the *salon* with the tray of hot tea glasses in hand, she saw Widad coming toward her in the hallway. Just then the bathroom door opened and out came Halimah. Her timing put her face to face with Widad in the hallway.

Halimah was dressed and had her head completely covered in a towel and only a slit for her eyes showed any part of her face. She looked comical in a towel worn like a *tarha* and if the situation had not been serious, Mia would have laughed out loud.

"*Salaam aleykum,*" Halimah said through her towel, her voice muffled.

"*Aleykum wassalaam,*" Widad replied, looking perplexed.

Time froze: Halimah facing Widad with a towel hilariously wrapped around her face, Widad looking at Halimah, shocked and confused, and Mia, trying to balance a tray of hot tea glasses while hiding her dismay at what might happen next.

Then time started again. Halimah walked away, toward the children's room, as if wearing a towel wrapped around her face was the most normal thing ever. Widad, still looking confused, just stood there staring at Halimah's back. Mia walked toward Widad, a big smile plastered across her face.

"Shall we have tea?"

"Who was that?" Widad asked, as Mia busied herself stirring sugar into each of the cups.

"Oh, that was a friend of mine," Mia answered vaguely.

"A friend of yours?" Widad asked, trying to get more information.

"Yes. How many spoons of sugar would you like?"

"Three, but is she Sudanese? Where did she go?"

Mia stared at the cups of tea, silently pleading for a way out. Michael sensed her tension and came to the rescue.

"Yusra! Come here! Tell me, how old are you? What is your favorite color? What new things do you think your father should sell in his store?"

Yusra was delighted at the attention and everyone enjoyed laughing at her answers to Michael's barrage of questions.

After half an hour of visiting, Widad leaned toward Mia. "I need to pray."

"OK, but I am sorry—I don't have a prayer mat for you."

"That's OK," she replied. "I can use a towel."

Mia showed Widad to the bathroom where she could perform the customary washing, and she fetched a bath towel from the bathroom shelf. Widad washed and then brought her towel down to the end of the hallway and positioned it so she could face Mecca, as all Muslims do when they pray. Mia wondered how she knew which direction to face.

To Mia's dismay, Widad set the towel just outside the same room that Halimah was hiding in. Widad stood at one end of the towel in her bare feet and began the ritual, looking from one shoulder to the other.

"*Salaam aleykum. Salaam aleykum.*" She proceeded with her prayer, bowing at the waist, standing, getting down on her knees, then leaning down to press her head against the floor and back up again.

The whole time Mia stood around the corner, out of sight, and prayed that Halimah would stay put and not come out of the door. Did Widad choose that location simply because she was trying to get close to the children's room and see who was inside? Was she trying to figure out where Halimah was? Would Halimah come out of the room, thinking she was safe? Mia tried to pray instead of worry, but it was hard.

Widad finished her prayer and folded up the towel, then put her shoes back on and walked back to the guest *salon.* Mia scurried back to join the others just ahead of Widad. When Widad re-entered the room, Mia looked up and smiled pleasantly as if nothing strange had happened.

After what seemed like an eternity, the Sudanese family stood up to say goodbye. Mia forced herself to be polite and take her time with the final greetings instead of rushing them out of the gate. Once they were gone, Mia breathed a sigh of relief.

⚜

A month turned into two months and there was still no safe alternative for Halimah. Mia marveled at Halimah's patience. Surely it was wearing thin.

"Teach me something about Sudanese Arab women," Mia said to Halimah.

The Sudanese girl thought for a few minutes. Then her eyes lit up.

"*Halawa!*"

"*Ha*—what what?"

"*Halawa*! Sudanese Arab women use something called *halawa*, or sugaring, to remove body hair. I'll make it and show you how to use it."

Halimah gathered supplies in the kitchen while Mia watched. She boiled water and added lemon and sugar until the mixture was like syrup. Then she poured it onto a cookie sheet to set. When it was cool she peeled the concoction off the tray and formed it into a sticky ball.

"You can store the ball in a clean jar in the refrigerator," Halimah said. "Now, come with me to the *salon* and I will show you how to use it."

Mia propped her leg up on the coffee table while Halimah kneaded the sticky ball until it was warm and supple in her hands. Next Halimah spread the *halawa* down a portion of Mia's leg. It felt warm and Mia relaxed, watching in fascination. Then, without warning, Halimah yanked the sugary substance off Mia's leg, ripping out hair, roots and all.

Mia yelped in surprise. Again and again Halimah spread out the mixture and ripped out the hair with expert speed. Mia felt like she was repeatedly skinning her knees and legs on rough pavement. She screamed, but she laughed too. She couldn't help it. It was funny and painful all at the same time.

"Sudanese girls, when they prepare to get married, remove all their body hair in this way," Halimah explained.

Mia stopped laughing and looked at her friend. "All of it?"

"All of it."

"You're kidding!"

"I'm not."

"Give me that!" Mia said playfully and grabbed the sticky ball away from Halimah. "No more *halawa!*"

Halimah laughed. "But feel your legs, aren't they smooth now?"

Mia rubbed her palm across her shin. It was true. They were incredibly smooth. Was it worth the pain? She wasn't convinced.

The car engine rumbled and then stopped as Michael pulled the vehicle into the driveway.

"Oh no! Michael is home from work."

"What's wrong?" Halimah asked.

"We've been busy with the *halawa,* and I didn't make anything for dinner."

"What about leftovers?"

"We ate them all for lunch."

Just then Michael walked in the house and set his briefcase down by the door. He looked tired.

"Hi, Michael," she said. "How was your day?"

"It was long," he replied.

"Michael, I'm sorry to say that I don't have anything planned for dinner."

"Oh," he said, sounding even more tired, "should I go get something for all of us? I could buy *shawarmas.*"

"That would be great. Thank you."

Michael turned around and walked outside to get back in the car. Ugh! Mia felt bad that she hadn't planned better.

After Michael was gone, Halimah turned and looked at Mia, her eyes wide. "I can't believe you did that. Will he be mad?"

"He's tired," Mia replied, "but he won't get mad."

"If my mother ever did that to my father, he would have hit her," Halimah said.

"Michael loves and respects me. We are like partners and sometimes one of us has to do more than the other and help out when a job is not done. We don't get upset about it usually."

"Like when Michael helped you wash the dishes, right?" Halimah asked.

Mia laughed at the memory. "Yes! Your first week here you couldn't believe Michael was helping me wash dishes!"

"I had never seen a man wash dishes before."

"There must have been a lot of strange things for you when you first came here."

Halimah nodded. "You are the first *khawadja* family I've ever known!"

Mia laughed. "Yes, I guess we are."

"I have learned a lot from you," Halimah said.

"I've learned a lot from you as well."

"Like *halawa!*" Halimah grinned.

"Well, yes, but more important things too. Like how to stand up for what you believe in."

"How long do you think it can last, Mia?" Halimah asked.

"How long can what last?"

"This." Halimah spread her arms out as if to indicate everything. "Me living here. It will not last forever. Someone will find out. How long can it last?"

"I don't know, Halimah."

❖ CHAPTER 27 ❖

Dear Mia,
Thank you for telling me more about your houseguest and her situation. Please tell her I said hello and that I am praying for her.

But I've also been worrying about it a lot lately. Don't you think it is too dangerous for you and Michael to be keeping a runaway like this? You need to consider your children as well. This is not safe.

Perhaps it is God's will for her to return home and be martyred for Jesus.

Love,
Mom

"Are you kidding me?" Mia paced the length of their bedroom after telling Michael the contents of the email. "What is Mom thinking?"

"Your mother is just worried about us, that's all, Mia."

"She is throwing the word *martyr* around like it's the easiest thing in the world! She may be able to throw Halimah to the wolves, but I cannot. I will not!"

"Mia." Michael's voice was calm. "Your mother doesn't understand this. She doesn't know that we are praying and seeking the Lord through all of this."

"She doesn't know that Halimah is like a daughter . . . or a sister . . . or . . . something. Halimah is family to us. How dare she say to send her home. I can't send Halimah home!"

"Mia, your mother wants you—wants us—to be safe. You have to give her that. And we want to do what the Lord guides us to do. If the Lord guides Halimah home, she'll go. Of that I have no doubt. It's OK if your mother doesn't understand."

"Well, I wish she did." Mia's anger melted into a pout.

Michael chuckled. "Don't worry. Something will work out."

"Well, I hope something works out before too long. It's going on three months now."

"We will just keep praying," Michael said, drawing her into an embrace.

Why had she ever doubted that he cared about her? And why had she ever wanted to leave Sudan? She would have missed Halimah altogether if she had gone home.

Mia noticed a new pattern in Halimah's schedule. She was staying up late into the night and using Mia's computer to visit Arabic chat rooms on the Internet. She discussed religion with Sudanese who lived in other countries. Halimah was bold in her witness to them. Michael had taught Halimah how to access the Internet through a virtual private network so that her location could not be discovered.

As she met new people, she and Mia would pray for them by name. Halimah uploaded information about Jesus so that her new friends could read and understand how He really was the Son of God. She had recently discovered that several Christian websites were blocked in Sudan so that Sudanese did not have access to the information. She was upset to see that her fellow countrymen were blinded and in bondage by what she considered propaganda being taught to them, just as it had been taught to her all her life. But Halimah had found a way to break free—to use the freedom of the Internet to tell people about freedom in Christ.

One night Halimah talked with a young man who had been held captive in a Sudanese *ghost house*. These houses were used to punish people who spoke out against the government or participated in protests, even peaceful ones. Mia knew these clandestine torture houses lurked somewhere in the corners of Khartoum, but she had never talked to anyone who had been in one.

Halimah and Mia were saddened by the things the young man had to endure at the hands of his torturers. Somehow, he had escaped and was living in Europe, but the memories still haunted him. Halimah told him about the healing power of Jesus. She became a safe listening ear to many Sudanese, like this man, and even to Saudis and other Arabs who found her on the Internet. Many of them were overcome by their questions, their past, their current situations, and felt they had nowhere to turn. Halimah guided them with Scripture and encouragement.

Michael and Mia marveled at how this young new believer in their home could touch and inspire so many people even when she herself was in hiding. Her gift of evangelism found an outlet on the Internet. Mia was proud of Halimah for refusing to wallow in self-pity.

Since she didn't go to sleep until four or five o'clock in the morning, she would sleep all morning. Mia didn't think this was a good idea, but the parental lines were blurry. Mia was Halimah's discipler, her surrogate mother, and the woman of the house. But, on the other hand, she was barely ten years older than Halimah. She did not want to treat Halimah like a child. Mia wanted her to have all the choices and freedoms she could have, since few were available to her.

Mia decided not to say anything to her about the late nights, but she missed having Halimah around during the mornings.

One night, Mia was sound asleep when there was a tap on the bedroom door. Mia opened the door and peered out. There was

Halimah. Her eyes were wide open and she had an excited look on her face. Was something wrong? Mia tiptoed out and closed the door quietly behind her, not wanting to wake Michael up.

"What's wrong, Halimah?" She whispered.

"Oh, Mia, it's so exciting! Remember Hamdi?"

Mia rubbed the sleep from her eyes and tried to focus. Who was Hamdi? She had no idea what Halimah was talking about and why this was important. What time was it anyway?

"No, who is Hamdi?"

"You remember . . . Hamdi! We have been praying for him. He lives in Saudi Arabia, and I have been chatting with him."

Mia remembered that they had been praying for a young man in Saudi Arabia. She nodded sleepily. "Oh yes, I remember. Is he OK?"

"Yes, he is fine. He is very interested in hearing more about Jesus! We made an appointment to meet again tomorrow, and I will give him more information. Mia, I think he might be ready to believe!"

Was that what she woke me up for? Couldn't that wait until the morning?

Mia looked into Halimah's eyes which were dancing with excitement. Mia tried to be happy too, but she was too frustrated at being woken up.

"Yes, that's good Halimah. OK, I'll see you tomorrow." Mia turned and stumbled back to bed, grumbling to herself.

The next morning during Mia's prayer time, she felt sheepish about her reaction the night before. She should have been excited for Halimah and happy for Hamdi. Why was Mia more concerned about a full night's sleep than about a man's salvation? Couldn't she wake up and celebrate with Halimah without grumbling?

Lord, forgive me for being selfish.

Mia sighed. She needed to ask Halimah for forgiveness as well. Mia tried hard to be a good example for the young woman, but she was definitely not perfect. Halimah was getting it all: the good and the bad. Mia sincerely hoped she was learning from both and would not hold the bad against her.

Halimah found it very strange that Michael and Mia went to bed at ten o'clock every night. In Halimah's house, they rarely went to bed before midnight. Someone was watching television or visiting in the salon while Mama and Halimah bustled around in the kitchen, cleaning up dinner dishes or making tea for Father and his guests. The air was cooler in the evenings and neighbors enjoyed visiting then, as opposed to the scorching morning hours. Even Rania and Ali never went to sleep before eleven or twelve o'clock.

At first, Halimah tried to join Michael and Mia's schedule, but she couldn't fall asleep at ten o'clock. That wasn't the only different thing about living with this *khawadja* family. Their food tasted strange, and all Halimah heard all day long was English. As much as she wanted to become fluent in English, it seemed she never had a break from it. Sometimes she wanted to scream, "Speak Arabic!"

One night Halimah stayed up until three in the morning praying.

"Lord, I am very tired and I am wondering, couldn't You come now and take us all to heaven?"

But even as she formed the words, she knew it was not the time yet. The Lord was patient and wanted everyone to know about Jesus. Halimah thought about Samia, her dearest friend. She had been disappointed on the day she shared Jesus with Samia because Samia did not believe in the things Halimah said, even when Halimah thought she had been convincing.

She had to remind herself of Mansur's words: "It is not you, it is the Lord who draws people to Himself and saves them." She had not really understood those words until now. Mansur was talking about her family. Halimah was the only one in her family who was a believer. No one else. When her father and brother discovered her secret, well, her whole family and the whole neighborhood heard about Jesus.

Even Halimah's relatives who lived far away would hear about Jesus when they heard what had happened to her. When they heard, they would have to make a decision for themselves about the truth of Jesus. Halimah was sure that her neighborhood was covered with the news of her story and because of that, they had heard about Jesus too.

Maybe this is the way God will work in Sudan. He will spread the news about Jesus through situations like mine.

Three months turned into four. Still Mansur gave no news about a safe place for Halimah to go. Mia imagined all this waiting was a test of endurance for Halimah, who said she had been so busy and social when she lived at home.

One evening Mia joined Halimah on the veranda. "It's a nice evening tonight," she said as she sat next to her friend.

"Yes, it is. So tell me, how was your visit with Hanaan today?"

"Oh it was so-so, Halimah. I was thinking I'd better visit her before she came to visit me. I don't want her to find you here. But when I got there, our visit was so strange."

"What do you mean?"

"Well, she was so agitated, even downright belligerent. You know, before you came to live with us, I had an opportunity to share about Jesus with her. She seemed interested and I was so encouraged. But today I felt she was acting anti-American. She made ugly statements about the United Nations, assuming they were all American. I had to explain to her that 'UN' did not mean 'USA.' I tried to talk about Jesus with her, but she was on a rampage against America and everything became political. By the end of our visit, I was so discouraged."

"That's great, Mia!"

"What?" Mia raised her eyebrows. Had Halimah not been listening?

"She is right on track!"

"What do you mean?"

"Muslims follow a pattern in coming to Jesus. At least I did, as did the others in the house group I used to attend."

"What do you mean a pattern?"

Halimah leaned across the plastic table and grabbed her notebook. She began writing down numbers.

"A pattern, like this." She showed Mia the notebook. "Number one: No true knowledge of Christianity. Muslims know only what they see of Christianity from a distance. They assume Christians are just like the Americans they see on television shows. They see Sudanese Christians wearing tight clothes and sitting next to boys on benches outside of churches. These are wrong in Islam and they think badly of Christians, supposing that all Christians act like the few they have seen.

"Number two: Something happens that makes a Muslim interested in Christianity. For me it was reading the Bible and also the miracles that were happening in my life. But it could be other things too, like dreams. They become interested.

"Number three: they begin to learn more about Jesus and become very excited and very eager to learn more.

"Number four: as the Holy Spirit begins to work in their hearts, drawing them to Himself, they become nervous or scared. The old nature does not want to give up its hold on their life. They become irritable or argumentative about Jesus and the Bible. They are trying to find a reason why it is not true. But they will not find a reason, because it is the Truth! If they finally accept the truth, they will move on to number five: believing in Jesus."

"You see, Mia," Halimah pointed her pen to the number four, "this is where Hanaan is. She is just following the pattern. She is actually very close!"

"Wow." Mia looked at the pattern. "I will pray for her every day."

The women continued sitting on the veranda, enjoying the cool evening air. They listened to the hustle and bustle out on the streets. The extra traffic noise was from some event going on at the nearby Manara Club. The Manara Club was one of many in the city, a venue that was rented out for weddings, graduations, birthdays, or any other big event that required lots of space. Sure enough, before long the music cranked up, and they could hear a party of some sort.

Halimah was quiet. She looked like she was listening and thinking. Then she walked toward the front gate, still listening to the music and the announcer on the microphone. Mia followed Halimah to the gate. Halimah turned to Mia, her eyes filled with tears.

"What is it?" Mia asked.

"It is my graduation ceremony," she replied. "I was on the graduation committee and we were planning for invitations and decorations and location. Obviously, they chose the Manara Club . . . " Her voice trailed off.

They walked back toward the house in silence and then sat together on the cement steps leading up to the veranda. "They can't imagine that I am right here!" she said, spreading her arms out. "I'm just down the street from all my friends and not one of them knows." Tears ran down Halimah's cheeks in a silent cry. "In one day," she whispered, "in one day, Mia, my whole life changed."

CHAPTER 28

"I have good news for you, Halimah," Michael announced as he stepped in the front door. Halimah and Mia were sitting at the dining room table, drinking tea and talking. Mia had made a coconut custard pie, one of Halimah's favorites, and they were savoring the warm slices.

"What's the news?" she asked.

"Well, Mansur thinks he has found a way for you to get out of the city and go south."

"Really?" Halimah searched his eyes to see if he was joking. But this was nothing to joke about. It had been seven months since Halimah had received any sort of a lead on a safe place.

"Mansur wants to come to the house tomorrow afternoon to explain everything to you. If you agree, then you will leave this weekend."

"Wow, Halimah! This weekend is just a few days away," Mia exclaimed.

"Where will I go?" Halimah asked Michael.

"Well, of course, Mansur will tell you all the details tomorrow, but he knows of a leader from a church in Southern Sudan who is leaving soon to return home. He has agreed to let you ride in his car if Mansur will help to pay the rent on the car."

"Southern Sudan? What will I do there?" Halimah knew that Southern Sudan was not a necessarily good place for an Arab girl from the North. In addition to the racial tension, there was also religious tension. Southern Christians would not readily believe an Arab Northerner who claimed to have converted from Islam.

"I guess I just didn't expect the end of your time here to come so abruptly," Mia said.

"I guess I never expected to have to go south," Halimah said.

Mansur arrived the next day and explained the details. The man who would take her was not from the same network of house churches, but from a different denomination. The risk seemed worth it to the leaders of Mansur's church, though, because the longer Halimah stayed with the American family, the more likely she would be found by someone.

Mansur had arranged for the man to rent a vehicle and driver and arrive early Friday morning, just before dawn. They hoped that in the predawn light, they would make it safely past any checkpoints leading out of the city. It would be a long, hard drive, but by nightfall Halimah would be far from the capital city and much closer to safety. The following day they would drive further south until they finally crossed into Southern Sudan.

Halimah only had two days to prepare. Mia found a large duffel bag that she didn't need and Halimah packed her clothes in it. She made a list of things she wanted for the trip and Mia went to the store for her. They didn't know what she would be able to buy in the South. Maybe the place she was going was remote.

Mia bought extra toiletries and snacks for her to take along. She would need a familiar taste. Halimah packed all the Bibles and commentaries she had gathered over the months along with her journals and some pens. Before long, her duffel bag was full.

On Thursday afternoon, Beth came to bid Halimah farewell. That evening, the family prayed together and the three children hugged Halimah goodbye. Mia fought back tears. Halimah had become the kids' favorite auntie, and she knew they did not really understand what was going on.

Friday, before it was light, a white SUV pulled into the driveway. The church leader was not in the car, but he had sent the driver to fetch Halimah.

"I guess this is it," Mia said, eyeing the car. She hugged Halimah goodbye, too numb for tears. Michael loaded her bag in the car and Halimah adjusted her scarf and sunglasses so that none of her face was seen. Then she climbed into the car.

And just like that she was gone.

Halimah felt strange to be outside the gates of Michael and Mia's home. It had been months since she had seen anything or anyone other than what came through their front gates. She pulled her *tarha* tightly around her face and adjusted the sunglasses over her eyes. She could see only dark shadows in the predawn light.

She sat nervously in the back seat of the SUV and peered out the windows while the driver, a Southern Sudanese, drove quietly. She was told that they were to go to the house of the church leader who was traveling south and pick him up, along with his wife.

It was going to be a long trip and would be the first time Halimah had ever spent time alone with Southern Sudanese people. She struggled to push away her prejudiced thoughts. She'd been raised to look down on the darker tribes of Southern Sudan, but now they were her only hope.

After fifteen minutes of driving, the vehicle stopped in front of what looked like a large compound. It must have been a church property of some sort. Perhaps the church leader lived there. After a few minutes, a man came out and got in the front seat next to the driver. He was tall and very black. He wore an olive green safari suit and carried a small black brief case.

"Good morning," he said. His tone was curt. The car began to pull away.

"What about your wife, Sir?"

"She is not coming after all," the man said. Halimah gulped. Was she going to travel alone with these two men all the way to Southern Sudan? The driver steered the car down the bumpy residential road and made a few more turns before stopping in front of another house. Halimah could not see what sort of house it was because of the privacy wall that surrounded it, like most houses in Khartoum. The passenger got out and went inside.

Halimah leaned toward the driver and asked, "Where are we?"

"We will be leaving soon," he said.

But they did not leave soon. The driver got out and leaned against a tree near the car, and Halimah waited in the back seat.

After what seemed an eternity, the man returned with his briefcase and some sacks in his hands. He loaded them in the back of the SUV where Halimah's duffel bag was and both men hopped back in the front seat. The passenger muttered something to the driver, but Halimah could not hear what he said. Was it even Arabic? Perhaps he was speaking in a Southern dialect.

Halimah coughed, hoping to remind them of her presence in the backseat, but they acted as if she was not there. Halimah felt the muscles in her jaw tighten. Something was not right.

The sun was beginning to rise, casting light on the scenes around them. Halimah recognized this part of town. It did not seem at all like they were heading out of town.

Perhaps we are going to pick up some more bags or another passenger.

Halimah leaned toward the front seat. "Will we be picking up another passenger?"

Neither the passenger nor the driver turned around. The passenger spoke. "We will head out of town soon."

Halimah leaned back in her seat and tried to relax. It was impossible. She looked out of the window and her eyes widened behind the smoky lenses of her sunglasses. They were entering the bus station near a market that Halimah used to shop at often. Her stomach churned. What were they doing? These men knew that Halimah's family was searching for her. Surely they knew that a bus station was not a good place to take her. Halimah's heart beat wildly. If she was recognized by anyone in that station, they would certainly call her family, and it would be easy to track her down. There would be no escaping a second time.

It was still early. The station was not as busy as it would be in the next hour or so. Still, most of the shops were open, and many commuters were coming and going in the dirty arena of buses, carts, and rickshaws.

The passenger did not turn around, but said over his shoulder, "The plans have changed. We will be riding the bus. I will get our tickets now, and we will leave as soon as the bus is ready." Then he turned to the driver and said something in a low tone that she didn't understand. The SUV stopped suddenly. The passenger jumped out, removed his briefcase from the back of the vehicle, and walked away.

Halimah was too shocked to speak. She stared at the scene around her, terrified. Her throat was dry, while beads of sweat gathered on her forehead.

Had Mansur changed the plan with this man and forgotten to tell her? No, he would not do that. Did Michael and Mia trick her? No, she couldn't believe that, not after seven months of living in their home. Was this man even the right one? He had to be. But surely he knew it was not safe for Halimah to ride the bus. Buses stopped at every checkpoint along the way. If Halimah wasn't discovered on the bus itself, she would surely be discovered at the very first stop. Passengers were often required to show their papers, and she had no identification at all.

Halimah tried to fight the panic that was welling up in her. She looked out the window and, to her dismay, saw the elder brother of Howeida. He was just leaving a shop that sold soft drinks and looked as if he was heading toward one of the buses.

Halimah needed to do something. She needed to get out of there.

She leaned toward the driver and pleaded, "Sir, I need to make a phone call. Please, can I borrow your phone?"

Not everyone had cell phones, but Halimah hoped that this driver had one. She would call Michael and Mia. She needed to tell them that she was in danger.

"I'm sorry," the driver replied, "I don't have any minutes left on my phone."

Halimah barely heard anything except for the word *phone* and she was overcome with relief that he had one. That was something, at least. But she needed to use it before the passenger came back. *Come on Halimah. Think quickly.*

"I will pay to put minutes on it."

Halimah searched through the small bag she carried with her in the back seat. In it were snacks, a bottle of water, and a wallet that Mia had given her. Pulling out some bills, Halimah handed them up to the driver.

"Please, Sir, can you buy some minutes for your phone and then let me use it?"

To her relief, the driver agreed. He took the money and got out of the car to find a shop that would sell minutes. Halimah leaned back in the seat and rested her head, eyes closed. She tried to breathe normally, but her heart was racing.

Please, Lord, help me get out of this bus station safely.

The driver returned with his phone and a new phone card. He fumbled around trying to enter the code for the additional minutes. The battery of his phone was running low and beeped a warning.

"I don't have my glasses," he grunted, "I cannot read the numbers on the card."

Halimah looked out the window of the car. It was getting later and more people were filling up the station. Though it was a station that ran some out-of-town buses, it also ran quite a few buses within the city limits. Several of Halimah's university friends used this station to catch buses to the campus. She didn't want to see anyone else that she knew, but she couldn't stop herself from staring at all the people.

"I can't get it to work," the driver said in frustration. He handed the phone and card to Halimah. "If you can enter the number, you can make a phone call."

"Thank you," she replied and grabbed the phone quickly.

She had no other plan for what to do if she could not call for help. The man who was getting their bus tickets—if that was really where he went—was obviously not trying to help her. This plan had to work.

Halimah closed her eyes and said a silent prayer for help again. Then she entered the numbers. The code worked and the phone finally had a credit, although it continued to beep its "low battery" warning. Then Halimah's heart sank. Who was she going to call? In her desperation to find a phone, she forgot that she didn't have any phone numbers with her. She wanted to cry, but the adrenaline now pumping in her veins would not allow her the luxury.

She had to think of something. Her life depended on it. Then she remembered. Before she went to live with Michael and Mia, she had memorized the name and number on the paper that the university professor had given her. She didn't know who it was at the time—just a man who could teach her about Jesus. But, of course, it was Mansur's number. And now, more than seven months later, she still remembered it.

Halimah punched in the numbers quickly and waited anxiously as it rang. When Mansur answered, she told him where she was.

"He betrayed you, Halimah. You have to get out of there."

"Help me, Mansur!" was all she could say.

"I am out of town at a church training in another city. I will give you the number for Michael and Mia."

Halimah listened to the number, willing herself to remember it. Then she hung up quickly since the battery on the phone was almost dead. She frantically pressed in the numbers for Michael and Mia's home phone before she could forget. The phone rang.

Halimah looked around the bus station. The passenger was nowhere to be seen. Perhaps he was still waiting in line for bus tickets, but she knew he would not be much longer. *Pick up! Pick up!*

Michael answered the phone and again, Halimah quickly blurted out her situation. Michael remained calm and assured her that everything would be all right. She could hear the tension in his voice, but she clung to the calmness of his words.

"Hang up, Halimah, and wait for me. I will call you right back."

Halimah obeyed. She squeezed her eyes tightly shut and prayed for extra life for the phone battery.

CHAPTER 29

It was very early in the morning when Halimah left. Michael and Mia had gone back to bed to sleep a bit longer. They woke up around six-thirty to get ready for the day. Corey, Annie, and Dylan, too young to appreciate the possibilities of a weekend morning to sleep in, were up and ready to play.

After a breakfast of leftover banana bread, Mia pulled out the box of Legos and spread the colorful bricks into a large round Sudanese eating tray. This served as the perfect toy holder. Its edges were just high enough to contain all the little pieces, and it was also large enough to spread them out and sort through them.

All three kids and Mia gathered around the tray and began building inventions. This kept them entertained until mid-morning which meant that, as long as Mia halfway looked like she was playing too, she could sip her coffee and relax. She talked and laughed with them, but inside all she could think of was Halimah. She prayed for safety for Halimah as she fled the city. Surely she was several hours outside of Khartoum by now and past all of the main checkpoints.

At nine o'clock the house phone rang. Mia was on the floor with the Legos and the boys. Michael answered it. He talked for just a few moments in Arabic and Mia knew immediately that something was wrong.

"We have a problem," Michael said.

Mia's heart skipped a beat. *A problem? Halimah should be far away by now. It couldn't be about her.*

"What's wrong?"

"Halimah called from the bus station."

"The bus station? What bus station? She's supposed to be halfway to Southern Sudan by now!"

"Apparently the church leader took the money that Mansur gave for the car rental and is going to buy bus tickets instead. She is in the bus station now but is still in the car. She is afraid if she gets out of the car she will be found."

"Michael, what can we do?"

"I don't know. I have to think. Let me call Mansur."

Mia grabbed Corey's hands. "Corey, we have to pray."

"OK, Mom," he said, and he grabbed Annie's hand. "Let's pray, Annie."

Dylan threw down his Lego pieces and folded his hands.

"Oh Lord, give us wisdom," Mia said, "Please protect Your daughter Halimah. Please don't let anyone find her and please help that driver to be kind to her."

Meanwhile, Michael finished talking to Mansur.

"It is not safe for you to be seen at the bus station. The best thing would be to try to talk the driver into bringing her back," Mansur had advised.

Michael called Halimah and asked to speak to the driver. Finally, he hung up and then headed to his briefcase to retrieve his keys. He talked over his shoulder while doing so. "OK, the driver has agreed to drive her out of the bus station and meet me at a neutral place. But he says the man who hired him is already gone. He must have decided to ride the bus on his own and just pocket the money."

Mia hurried to open the gate for Michael as he pulled the Land Rover out and sped away. She paced the floor and tried to calmly pray, forcing herself to think of anything besides what would happen if Halimah were caught and turned over to the police—or returned to her home.

Half an hour later, Michael pulled into the driveway with

Halimah in the backseat. Mia ran out to meet them and as soon as Halimah stepped out of the car, Mia embraced her as if they had been apart for a year. Mia quickly ushered Halimah into the safety of the house. She didn't want Halimah ever to leave the house again.

❧ ❧

Mansur was out of town until the end of the week, and they couldn't talk about the problem over the phone. They were stuck in waiting mode, just as they had been for seven months.

After Halimah was home safely, she told Michael and Mia her story. They prayed and thanked the Lord for watching out for her. The fact that the driver was willing to let her use his phone and then take her to Michael was nothing short of a miracle. But their relief that Halimah was safe was overshadowed by the many questions that were unanswered.

What happened to the church leader? Had he boarded a bus on his own and left Halimah and the driver sitting in the station? They only knew that the man had taken money from Mansur and apparently run away. The driver said he had even left a couple of bags of clothes in the SUV.

What would have happened if Halimah had been recognized in the bus station? Halimah said she probably would have been taken to her family who would have immediately sent her to the *khalwa*. Certainly, she said, they would not have allowed her to stay in Khartoum. They would have hidden her away somewhere so she could not escape again.

Was Halimah safe now that this man who had betrayed her knew where she lived? What about the driver? Would he report her to the police?

❧ ❧

Mia saw that Halimah's shoulders drooped and her eyes were heavy. She must be exhausted. Michael hauled her duffel bag back into her bedroom, and she changed back into a housedress and went to sleep. Mia busied herself entertaining the kids and planning lunch. She did all the things she would normally do on a Friday, except that she kept thinking about the near tragedy. Halimah had narrowly escaped disaster.

The following weekend, Mansur came to visit at night. Mia was glad he came to the house. She knew it was risky that way, but Halimah was greatly encouraged when she saw him. He was, after all, her pastor. After Mia brought the glasses of water and then the tea and a plate of bananas, the women sat down with Michael and Mansur and Halimah told about all that had happened on the previous Friday.

Mansur did not have answers for the man's behavior. He said he would try to contact him, but the infrastructure down south was not well developed and sometimes it was hard to get phone calls to go through. He was surprised and saddened that the man had stolen the money.

Mia was too, but she was angry that the man put Halimah's wellbeing at risk to do it. What sort of Christian would do that? How could someone be that self-seeking? Mia wanted to pray that the Lord would punish that man.

"It is not good for Halimah to stay here much longer," Mansur said. "Now that the church leader and his driver know she is here, it is time for her to move. I will continue looking for a safe way for her to leave."

Mansur thanked them for the tea and made his exit. He slipped away into the night and Michael, Mia, and Halimah slipped back into their routine. Halimah did not fully unpack her duffel bag, Mia noticed. She kept most of her things packed and the bag shoved under her bed.

❖ CHAPTER 30 ❖

*M*ia agreed with Halimah that it was best to act as if she would be traveling soon. Where the Lord had once given them a peace about waiting, He now had given them a sense of urgency for Halimah to leave. They prayed for a miracle, and they knew Mansur was looking for a solution.

The failed attempt had come up so quickly that Halimah really hadn't had much time to prepare. She wanted to be more prepared for the next time and, in the days that followed, she spent some time on the Internet saying goodbye to the people she had met in the chat rooms. Mia baked Halimah's favorite things one last time: coconut custard pie and banana bread.

Mansur encouraged Halimah to think of a new name to use once she left Khartoum. She would need to have a new identity. What a strange feeling it must have been for Halimah: to change her name and her identity when deep inside she was still the same Halimah she had always been. Of course, she was redeemed now, and Mia supposed her new name could represent her new identity in Christ.

Mia and Halimah discussed several names. Mansur said she needed to choose a name that was not clearly Muslim or Christian. The first name was not as important as the second name.

The second name, in Sudan, was the name of one's father, the third name was the grandfather, and so on, all the way up the family tree. Halimah said that Sudanese Arabs could tell what tribe a person was just by the names of their fathers and grandfathers.

Halimah chose an Arab second name and a third name from a southern tribe. She was stumped on her first name, though.

"How about Harriett?" Mia offered. "That's a non-Muslim name and it is close to your real name!"

"No way!" Halimah said and laughed.

"How about Mia, like Mom?" Corey asked, happy to help choose a new name for his adopted big sister.

"I love your mom very much, Corey," Halimah replied. "But I think a different name will keep us all from getting confused!"

Finally, Halimah chose *Sara*. That was a good name that could be acceptable to Muslims and Christians alike.

Halimah stayed another month before Mansur came up with a new plan. From the beginning, this plan seemed to be a much better idea to everyone than the first one.

Mansur and Michael knew a man that could help. He had attended many meetings at the international church, and Halimah met him once at the house prayer group that she had attended when she was still at home. This man was from a southern tribe and was going home to visit his family for a few weeks. He was riding with a family who said there would also be room for Halimah in the vehicle. He did not ask for any money. Because it was a group traveling together, he did not expect much individual scrutiny at the checkpoints.

"What do you think, Halimah?" Mansur asked after he shared the plan.

"I think it is good. I think we should do it."

Halimah would travel in a week's time.

Mia could hardly believe it. Here they were again: getting Halimah's bag packed, running to the store to buy her last-minute items, baking some snacks for her to take for the long trip, and taking final pictures together. Before Mia was ready for it, the day had arrived. How strange it felt to be re-enacting what had, once before, turned into a near-disaster.

The vehicle came early in the morning, just before dawn. Halimah was wearing the same traveling clothes she had worn on that previous travel day, complete with a *tarha* and sunglasses. But this time, their mutual friend and all his traveling companions arrived to meet her, introducing themselves in a friendly way and helping her into the car. Her bag fit nicely in the back, but the seating situation was very tight.

Michael, Mia, and their three kids smiled and waved and wished them well. The car backed out of the driveway and slipped away down the dark street.

Mia kept listening for the phone to ring, but it didn't. Was that a good sign? Finally, mid-morning, they received a call from Halimah's traveling companions to say that they had made it out of the city with no problem and were safely on their way.

"What wonderful news!" Mia forced herself to say.

The next day they called one last time to say they were nearing the border of Southern Sudan and that she was almost to her destination.

Mia felt numb. Halimah was truly gone. Mia had not given much thought to what life after Halimah would look like. For eight months Mia's life had revolved around Halimah. What would she do now? She had poured herself into Halimah for the better part of a year. She gave up friendships, projects, and personal interests—and she had loved doing it. Mia felt honored to stand side by side with a persecuted believer.

But what was she to do now? Was she still a part of Halimah's life? Did she still have a role to play in Khartoum?

Michael and Mia's daily life, carefully adjusted to fit Halimah in, now abruptly changed back to "normal," yet it did not feel normal at all. Michael had not been home alone for eight months. Now he was free to come home whenever he pleased. Mia could also come and go as she pleased, without worrying about what Michael would do or where he would go.

When someone knocked on the gate, Mia no longer looked for police boots at the bottom of the gate or wondered what she might say if a policeman showed up. With the absence of these things, Mia relaxed. She felt the tension flowing out of her over the following days.

But also, when Mia came home from visiting with Hanaan, she had no one to share it with. Michael was happy to hear her experiences, of course, but Halimah had such wise insights into what a Sudanese woman was thinking. Mia had no one to sit with on the veranda, to laugh and talk about everything and nothing in particular.

Corey, Annie, and Dylan missed Halimah too. She had been there to play with them or hug them or get them a snack when they were hungry. Halimah was part of the family, and it didn't feel right not to have her there.

The days wore on and they settled into a new pattern: life after Halimah. Mia didn't like it at first, but it was much better for Halimah to be free. And as Mia thought over the eight months of hiding Halimah, she was overwhelmed with a spirit of gratitude.

A year earlier, Mia had been a young housewife and mother, trying to make sense of her life in an Arab man's world, wondering why she was working hard to make a life for her family in Sudan, of all places. Mia had been jealous of her single friend, Beth, who she thought had much more to offer. And she was frustrated at feeling hidden behind the cement walls that surrounded her daily life.

Yet, all along, God had a special plan for her. He needed someone just like Mia to be available for Halimah. He needed a woman who was free to stay home to take care of Halimah's needs. He needed a secluded house, set away from the curious eyes of the community. He wanted to use someone like . . . her!

Perhaps the future was not bleak after all. Michael and Mia had discovered ways to reach out to families together. Along with the kids, they had been visiting Habiib and Nahla as well as Abbas and Widad. When Michael was tied up at work, Mia didn't mind as much because she would often take the children to play at Hanaan's house.

Halimah had assured Mia that Hanaan was very close to accepting Christ. Now that Halimah was gone, Mia could invite her to come for a visit. Would that be the time she would finally believe in Jesus? Any one of Mia's Sudanese friends could be secretly wanting to learn more about Jesus. Why had Mia not realized it before?

Dear Mom,

Our houseguest is gone now. It is hard letting go of her, but she has much more to write in her amazing life story. I am grateful to have been a small part of her life because she has become such a big part of mine. Michael and I have no doubt that she will go on to do great things for the Lord.

I know you'll say that Michael and I were brave to do what we did. But it was never about being brave. It was never about whether hiding this young woman was a smart idea or foolish. And, I discovered, it was never about me. It was always about God. It was always about God's faithfulness: His faithfulness to her and His faithfulness to us.

There was a point when I didn't think Sudan was worth it. You know what? I've discovered it's true. Sudan is not worth it. But Jesus is. Because Jesus is worth everything. And that's all that matters.

With love,

Mia

✧ CHAPTER 31 ✧

*M*ia sat in the open garden of a coffee shop sipping a latte. It had been three months since Halimah had moved to South Sudan, and she was eager to hear news from her. That morning she had received a text on her phone from an unknown number. *Meet me at Khartoum Coffee Shop at 10 today. I have a message from Sara.*

As she waited, Mia couldn't help but wonder if it was a trap. What if Halimah's family had discovered her new name? No, she had to believe that everything was all right. The Lord was in control.

Mia glanced around the garden. This was a coffee shop frequented by foreigners and upper-class Arabs. Mia watched a table full of college-age students. The girls and boys were flirting and laughing. Any one of those girls could have been Halimah a year ago. Mia wondered if any of those students were secretly reading a Bible.

As Mia was drinking the last of her coffee, a young man walked toward her. His smile was bright, his white teeth contrasting with his black skin. He was well-dressed and walked confidently.

"Mia?" he asked as he approached her table.

"Yes," Mia said, standing.

"I'm Daniel." He shook her hand. His English was impeccable, though it carried a hint of an African accent. "May I sit here?"

"Of course!" Mia gestured to the chair across from her.

"I have a letter for you from our sister Sara." Daniel reached into his pocket and pulled out an envelope. He slid it across the table toward Mia.

Immediately, Mia recognized the handwriting. *To My Sister Mia*. Tears flooded Mia's eyes.

"How is she?"

Daniel smiled. "She is doing very well. She sends you her love."

"How do you know her?"

"Sara now works for our organization in the South. We help the many refugees who live there. Some of them speak Arabic, but you may know that English is used quite a bit down in the South. Her English is quite good. I assume we have you to thank for that?"

Mia laughed. "Well, Sara is a smart woman. Oh, I'm so sorry . . . would you like some coffee?"

"Oh no, thank you. I have to go. I am only in Khartoum for one day. I'm on my way to Europe actually, to raise money."

"All right. It was nice to meet you. Thank you for the letter."

"My pleasure," Daniel said as he stood. "God bless you."

"You too," Mia said. She watched the man leave the garden area and hail a rickshaw that was driving by.

Mia looked down at the envelope. A message from Halimah. Finally! She ripped the sealed envelope and lifted out the folded paper. A grin spread across her face as she saw the pictures drawn in all the margins. There were pictures of animals and trees, birds and fish. At the top of the paper Halimah had written, "These pictures are for Corey, Annie, and Dylan. These are the beautiful things I see each day in South Sudan. It is very different from Khartoum!"

Mia looked at each picture in the margin, savoring the moment. Then she began to read the letter.

Dear Michael and Mia,

I am doing well and our God is providing everything I need. At first it was very hard for me to live in South Sudan and to rely on the help of people from African tribes. I think it was very hard for the people here to trust me, an Arab. But God has made a way for me and now I have found a job with an organization that helps refugees. I can play with the children and I also help with translation.

I don't know how long I will have this job, but I am trusting in God to help me with all of my needs now and in the future.

Thank you for giving me a safe place to live and for teaching me all about how to live in a way that pleases Jesus.

I will always think of you as my big brother and big sister in Christ. Thank you for standing by my side.

Please continue to pray for my family. I hope one day that they too will believe.

Your Sister,
Sara

AFTERWORD

While the story of Halimah is written as fiction, many people in the Muslim world today have similar experiences to Halimah's.

During the time I lived in Africa and the Middle East, I was privileged to meet many heroes of the faith who will, for the most part, remain unknown while here on earth. Their stories are untold, but their hearts are steadfast. There are others who did not hold fast to Jesus. Their stories end sadly for now, but redemption is available for those who return.

Halimah could have been from any country that abides by the laws of Islam, but I chose to write the setting in Northern Sudan because Sudan holds a special place in my heart.

Irony reigns over Northern Sudan. Just as the desert surrounding Khartoum is beautiful and terrible all at the same, beauty in Sudan displays itself against a backdrop of hardness and harshness.

The women of Sudan are as tough on the inside as they are beautiful on the outside. Swirling designs of black henna cover feet that are calloused from years of labor in the home. Sandalwood and incense, mixed with perfumes, cover the smell of sweat and body odor from cooking over a hot stove or cradling a feverish child.

Sudan is tough, and Sudan is beautiful. Most people never get to experience it. I did, and I wanted to share it with you.

WorldCrafts^{SM} develops sustainable, fair-trade businesses among impoverished people around the world. Each WorldCrafts product represents lives changed by the opportunity to earn an income with dignity and to hear the offer of everlasting life.

Visit WorldCrafts.org to learn more about WorldCrafts artisans, hosting WorldCrafts parties and to shop!

WORLDCRAFTS^{SM}
Committed. Holistic. Fair Trade.
WorldCrafts.org 1-800-968-7301

WorldCrafts is a division of WMU®.

Great fiction that spurs outreach!

Beyond I Do
$15.99
978-1-59669-417-0

When Dawn Breaks
$15.99
978-1-59669-423-1

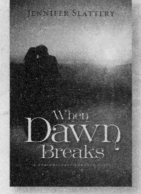

Download free book club discussion guides
at NewHopeDigital.com!

Available in bookstores everywhere. For information about other
books by this author, visit NewHopeDigital.com.